U700

Anders stared at the gun. 'I've got nothing to lose, have I? If I'm caught before I plant the bomb, the British will hang me. If I'm caught afterward, they'll hang me anyway. And if I manage to escape to Ireland after destroying the U-boat, the German navy will hang me after the war.'

'Very likely,' Kretschmer observed.

Anders smiled thinly. 'Well, at least I know where I stand.'

James Follett
U700

Mandarin

A Mandarin Paperback

U700

First published in Great Britain 1979
by Weidenfeld & Nicolson Ltd
This edition published 1989
Reprinted 1990, 1992
by Mandarin Paperbacks
Michelin House, 81 Fulham Road, London SW3 6RB

Mandarin is an imprint of the Octopus Publishing Group,
a division of Reed International Books Ltd

Copyright © 1979 James Follett

Photoset by Rowland Phototypesetting Ltd
Bury St Edmunds, Suffolk
Printed in Great Britain
by Cox & Wyman Ltd, Reading, Berks.

British Library Cataloguing in Publication Data

Follett, James, *1939–*
U700
I. Title

ISBN 0-7493-0035-3

For my wife Christine

Part One

1

Death was lying in wait for the convoy straggler.

The grey, rust-streaked, silent hull lay stopped on the surface – water dripping from its periscope standards and jumping wire with the same regular rhythm as the heavy metallic throb of the approaching ship's engines. Inverted golden horseshoes gleamed on either side of the conning tower. Down below, the waiting men stood silently by the torpedo tube that contained the U-boat's next-to-last torpedo. The hydrophone operator in the control room, headphones clamped over his ears, gave the doomed merchantman's course, range, and speed to the inscrutable man standing behind him, answering the U-boat commander's questions in a steady voice and without turning around. If he was aware of the expressionless eyes boring into the small of his back, he gave no sign.

There was a sudden movement in the control room as the commander climbed the steel rungs that led up to the attack kiosk in the conning tower. The hydrophone operator sensed the sudden relaxing of tension. Someone even made a quick joke.

The four lookouts on the U-boat's bridge studiously kept their eyes pressed to their binoculars as they stared into the fog. They didn't need the pungent whiff of a cheroot to tell them that the new arrival on the bridge was their commander. One of them, bolder than his mates, risked a glance at the gaunt figure. The movement caused the lookout's oilskins to squeak. The commander scowled but said nothing. The four men sensed his displeasure and did their best to stand absolutely still. The sound of the engines faded. For some seconds all that could be heard was the gurgle made by the swell as it vented through the deck casing drains when the U-boat lifted.

All five men heard the music at the same time: a choir singing in the fog.

Silent night, holy night.

An old German Christmas carol that now belonged to the world.

All is calm, all is bright.

By one of those tricks that fog plays with sound, the beat of the ship's engines reached the U-boat after the sound of the record.

The commander lifted his specially engraved Zeiss binoculars and trained them in the direction of the singing. They had been presented to him by Admiral Karl Doenitz – a gift from a grateful commander-in-chief of the U-boat arm to his topscoring 'ace'.

Round yon Virgin, mother and child.

The commander lowered his binoculars and stared into the fog as if he were willing the invisible ship to materialize. He muttered an order into the voice pipe.

Driven now by its electric motors, a small wave crept up the shark-like bow as the U-boat slipped silently and purposefully through the water.

There was no warning.

In an instant the happy party scene aboard the *Walvis Bay*, with the children excitedly opening their Christmas presents, became a nightmare of devastation and death as the cabin floor heaved upward and burst open like a giant, ruptured diaphragm.

The ship gave a sickening lurch and began to list as it

10

lost way. The port engine was torn from its shattered mountings. It smashed through the side of the ship as if the steel plates had been stretched tissue paper.

The bewildered radio operator clung desperately to his table in the tilting darkness. His instinct had been to join the stampede past the door of his radio shack, but he managed to shut out the cries of the terrified children who were being shepherded onto the deck by the two army nurses. He set the radio to 'transmit' and tapped out on the antique morse key: 'SSSS . . . SSSS . . . SSSS . . .' Submarine! Submarine! Submarine!

He gave the *Walvis Bay*'s call sign and position several times, but there was no answer from the rest of the convoy fifty miles ahead. He tried to raise a Newfoundland station but without success; the antenna wire was trailing uselessly in the water astern of the rapidly sinking ship.

A spot of light moved on the surface of the oil-black water. The searchlight beam was filled with swirling fog. There was the soft purr of electric motors. Accusing exhibits of unrestricted U-boat warfare swam briefly into the spotlight and moved on like actors lining up and bowing after a macabre finale: a teddy bear, a half-opened present, a man's leg.

The boatman's mate manning the searchlight wanted to switch the light off and shut out the horror. But there was the even more frightening, icy presence of the U-boat commander at his side, staring down at the water – saying nothing.

There was the sound of a child crying in the fog. The commander tensed. He tuned his head to locate the direction of the sound and issued a curt order into the voice pipe.

A crewman emerged on the bridge. He moved aft to the railed wintergarten deck and swung the 20 millimetre anti-aircraft gun down so that it was pointing at the water.

The commander issued another order.

U99 altered course toward the sound of the crying child.

The captain of the *Walvis Bay*, still wearing a Father Christmas costume that was now sodden and caked with oil, stood up in the lifeboat and motioned the army nurse to keep the crying child quiet. She gathered the six-year-old boy into her arms and whispered gently to him. His tears began to subside. The older children sensed the approaching danger and remained silent while peering with wide, frightened eyes into the fog. There were fifteen people in the lifeboat: the captain, the army nurse, and thirteen children who were evacuees from the London bombing.

The muffled purr of the approaching U-boat's electric motors grew steadily louder.

The captain saw the searchlight hardening in the fog and swore bitterly. He shivered with despair as he tried to swing the lifeboat around so that it presented a smaller target. But he was too late; the long, lean hull was sliding past the crowded, open boat. A conning tower swayed out of the fog. The U-boat's motors were thrown into reverse.

U99 stopped beside the lifeboat and bathed its occupants with the glare from the searchlight.

A voice spoke. Perfect English with hardly a trace of German accent.

'What ship?'

The captain clutched the oar as though it were a club. He suddenly felt foolish in the remnants of his costume. He shaded his eyes and thought he could discern the ghostly outline of a man behind the blinding light.

'What ship?' the voice repeated. There was a hint of impatience.

'Walvis Bay.'

'Cargo?'

The reply was flat and unemotional. 'Children.'

The searchlight moved to the pinched, frozen faces and came to rest on the nurse. She sensed a pair of eyes taking in every detail of her Queen Alexandra's Nursing Corps uniform.

There was movement on the U-boat's deck. Something soft landed at the nurse's feet. A blanket. Then another. She realized that two U-boatmen were lowering a crate into the lifeboat. One of the crew was holding out a small wooden box to the captain. He took it reluctantly. An older child overcame her fear and put her hand into the crate. She held up a bottle of brandy and a carton of cigarettes and looked disappointed.

The searchlight clicked out. The voice on the bridge gave an order in German. There was a growl of hidden starter motors followed by the explosive roar of the U-boat's diesel engines bursting into life. The captain groped for the torch and flashed it on the conning tower. The two men's eyes met for a few seconds. It was a face the *Walvis Bay*'s captain had seen before in newspaper photographs – the humourless, forbidding eyes and sardonic features dominated by a prominent, hawk-like nose. It was a face that embodied the inherent menace of the eagle that was the emblem of the Third Reich.

There was a bump as the crewmen fended the lifeboat away from the moving U-boat. The captain steadied himself. His torch dipped and illuminated the gleaming, inverted golden horseshoe on the side of the receding U-boat's conning tower. But the captain already knew who his adversary was. He stared at the lone figure that was being absorbed into the fog – his emotions a mixture of awe and astonishment.

'My God,' he whispered. 'That was Otto Kretschmer.'

He stared after the disappearing U-boat for some

seconds before opening the wooden box that had been handed to him by one of the U-boat's crew. Inside he found a compass. Coincidentally, its needle was pointing to the precise point where the fog had swallowed *U99*.

On *U99*, the crewman who had manned the gun was about to close the hatch when he noticed a piece of paper wrapped around one of the stanchions. He carefully removed it and laid it flat on the deck casing. It was a stencilled list of the names of the children and nurses aboard the *Walvis Bay*. The reverse had been used to make a Christmas card. It bore a crayoned message written in a child's awkward hand: MERRY CHRISTMAS AND A HAPPY 1941.

2

The ancient Citroën taxi bounced across the rain-polished cobbles and grated to a standstill outside the gate that led to Lorient harbour's U-boat quays. A bored stabsfeldwebel, wearing the duty gorget and chain of the military police, approached the taxi and took the offered papers from the passenger.

Lieutenant Bernard Anders – the photograph matched the anxious face: fair hair, a pale complexion. He noted the long legs that were virtually drawn up to the occupant's chin in the taxi's cramped interior.

The stabsfeldwebel stood back and waved the taxi through the gate and returned to his guard box with its cracks stuffed with shredded newspapers to keep out the biting February wind that blew with toothache ferocity off the Atlantic and into a man's bone marrow.

He had just made himself comfortable when another

new arrival turned up in a taxi. Typical, he thought. Too full of self-esteem to even consider sharing a taxi.

Another officer, perhaps younger than the first one. He had an eager, confident air. His uniform was an essay in perfection: his collar was spotless, and his cap, which he was managing to wear in the taxi, was at the correct angle. Everything about Sub-Lieutenant Richard Stein was well-ordered neatness. Everything, that is, except the ugly sweep of a sabre scar on his left cheek.

Bernard Anders found Pier Six and gazed down at his new boat. It was at least double the size of the 'canoes' he had completed his Baltic training on. Two engineers were preparing the submarine for combat by removing the fore and aft safety rails. A third was checking the 88-millimetre gun that dominated the foredeck. Anders lost count of the minutes as he absorbed every detail of the U-boat that was to become his home. He was roused by a pleasant voice behind him.

'Good afternoon.'

Anders turned. It was the well-scrubbed, smartly turned-out U-boat officer he had noticed on the train.

'I'm Sub-Lieutenant Richard Stein.' The sabre scar crinkled as he smiled. The knife-edge creases in his trousers were two vertical lines of uninterrupted perfection. His travel bags had been packed so that they were outwardly symmetrical. Anders was uncomfortably aware of his own awkward frame, which had been the despair of his proud mother when she had tried to alter his uniform to fit properly. He shook the offered hand, noticing that Stein's nails had been manicured.

'Lieutenant Bernard Anders,' Anders said, returning Stein's smile.

Stein nodded to the U-boat and brushed an invisible speck from his sleeve. 'Your new boat?'

'Yes.' Anders resented Stein's air of casual confidence. 'Which one?'

'*U700*.'

'Bad luck,' Stein said, gazing critically down at his gleaming toecaps.

Anders bridled. 'Oh?'

Stein looked up. 'But you've heard, of course? There was a piece on *U700* in *Das Reich*.'

'My parents don't take that newspaper,' Anders said, immediately regretting the reply, for it made him sound arrogant, which he hadn't intended.

The smile vanished from Stein's face. He picked up his travel bags and said coldly, 'There was an accident during her trials at Trondheim. I can't remember the exact details, but there was something about a citation for presence of mind shown by her captain. He'd be the best one to tell you.'

'What boat are you joining?' Anders asked as Stein turned to leave. 'I didn't mean to sound rude.'

'*U99*,' Stein said unsmilingly. But a hint of pride was in his voice as he added, 'Kretschmer's boat. She's due back tomorrow.'

Anders made no reply. Stein regarded him for a moment and then gave a faint smile that barely creased the polished tissue of his sabre scar.

'Good luck with *U700*, Lieutenant Anders. Let us hope that she's not going to be an unlucky boat.'

Captain-Lieutenant Hans Weiner was a large capable man in his late forties who had ably commanded a Type II training U-boat on the Baltic up to the summer of 1939. He had resigned himself to spending the war training recruits because he suspected that his age was against his receiving a front-line command. He was therefore surprised and grateful when his flotilla commander

16

informed him that he was to take delivery of *U700* from her builders. The accident that had deprived *U700* of nearly a quarter of her crew of forty men had happened during the second week of acceptance trials. After the necessary repairs had been completed, he had been ordered to sail for the newly captured port of Lorient in western France to await replacements. From his experiences on the Baltic with the large numbers of U-boatmen who failed to complete their training, he knew only too well that the chances of obtaining seasoned men to replace the nine men lost during the accident were slim.

He was sitting at his table adjoining the U-boat's wardroom, signing stores requisitions, when he heard someone descend the ladder into the control room. He drew aside his green curtain – the only concession to privacy that the commander of a Type VIIC U-boat was entitled to – and leaned into the companionway. An officer with an unfamiliar, loose-limbed build was peering through the sky periscope.

Weiner pulled his sweater straight and entered the control room. It was some moments before the new arrival noticed his presence. When he did, he straightened up from the periscope and smiled sheepishly.

'I didn't know anyone was aboard.'

Weiner studied the officer, noting the two gold rings on his sleeve. 'Are you Lieutenant Bernard Anders?'

'Yes. I have my papers.' Weiner took the sheaf of documents, glanced through them, and cursed inwardly. He had been promised an experienced first officer – one who had completed at least two war patrols – not a youngster hardly out of a cadet's uniform who had never poked his nose out of the Baltic's sheltered waters.

'Those papers are for Captain Weiner.'

'I'm Weiner.'

Anders' gangling frame came to immediate attention.

He saluted clumsily. 'I'm sorry, *kaleu*,' he said, using the customary abbreviation with which junior officers addressed a *Kapitanleutnant*.

Weiner waved the apology aside and gestured to the control room's interior. 'Well? What do you think of her?'

Anders smiled. He felt certain he was going to like Weiner. 'Impressive, kaleu. Bigger than the training boats.'

Weiner grunted. 'It will seem small enough after a few weeks on patrol.' He regarded Anders thoughtfully. 'So you're my new first watch officer?'

'I've served as an executive officer for three months, kaleu.'

Weiner grinned. 'On a Type II in the Baltic, eh?' He clapped Anders affably on the back. 'Come. I'll show you a real U-boat. Her teeth first.'

Weiner's powerful hand slapped one of the racked torpedoes affectionately. 'And this one is special, Mr Anders. Know what it is?'

Anders ducked his head under the overhead torpedo tube loading rails in the U-boat's bow torpedo room and peered at the long, black weapon. It looked the same as the other torpedoes except for the serial number suffix stencilled in neat white letters on the hemispherical warhead. He straightened up in surprise and nearly hit his head on the rails.

'A G7e warhead, kaleu.'

Weiner beamed. 'Right first time. But why the surprised expression?'

Anders stared at the sinister weapon gleaming dully in the light from the caged bulkhead lamps. Of its twenty-five-foot length, it was the jet-black warhead that held his attention; unlike the main body of the torpedo, the surface was smooth and highly-polished.

'I thought the magnetic warhead had been withdrawn from service, kaleu.'

'This is the Mark Two version,' Weiner replied, patting the warhead as if it were a dog. 'They say that all the bugs have been ironed out. Kretschmer, Schepke and Prien are sinking one ship per torpedo with these beauties.' Weiner's hand moved along the torpedo's curved flank to its propellers. 'And it's powered by electric motors instead of compressed air. No tell-tale bubble track.'

'The warhead appears to be made from a different type of metal, kaleu,' Anders said, unable to take his eyes off the gleaming hemisphere.

'It's a new type of "Wotan" steel developed by Krupp which allows the explosive in the warhead to build up to twice the pressure before it bursts. That way we get twice the explosive force for the same amount of explosive charge. But it's the fact that the warhead explodes underneath the target that does the real damage.'

Anders warmed to the older, almost fatherly man. Had Weiner been the kind of aloof senior officer he had experienced so far during his brief period in the *Kriegsmarine*, he would have lacked the courage to ask the question that was uppermost in his mind.

'What was the accident that happened to this boat, kaleu?'

Weiner spun around, the amiable expression gone. 'What accident?' he barked.

'I'm sorry, kaleu – I was told that during *U700*'s trials –'

'Oh that,' Weiner interrupted dismissively. He nodded to the group of four torpedo doors. 'Spot of trouble with Tube Three – faulty welding around the hinge.'

Anders understood exactly what that meant. 'You mean a door blew off?' he asked incredulously.

'Something like that,' Weiner said. 'But you don't want to be bothered with *U700*'s past misfortunes. It's her future successes that we're now concerned with.' He took Anders by the elbow. 'We'd better see about getting that uniform of yours sponged and pressed. Looks like you've slept in it. Can't have you meeting the admiral tonight looking like that.'

Anders froze. 'The admiral?'

'Why yes.'

'Admiral Doenitz?'

Weiner laughed. 'Of course. Unless Raeder has appointed a new U-boat Commander-in-Chief since this morning.'

A meeting with the legendary Karl Doenitz was the last thing Anders had bargained for. Weiner noticed his junior officer's alarmed expression and grinned broadly.

'If it's any comfort, I felt the same when I first met him at Wilhelmshaven some years ago. Tonight is *U700*'s precommissioning party. His Atlantic operations HQ is based here, so it's certain that he'll show up.'

3

The magnetic torpedo passed under the ore-laden ship and exploded directly beneath its keel.

Kretschmer and the other watchers on *U99*'s bridge saw a blinding sheet of flame leap high into the night sky. It had been *U99*'s last torpedo – fired from her stern tube.

The U-boat turned, bringing her main gun to bear so that the ship could be finished off with a mixture of incendiary and explosive shells. But the gun crew wasn't needed. As moonlight spilled across the sea through a gap in the cloud base, the astonished watchers saw the ore ship's masts tilt toward one another and slowly cross, like duellists' swords at the beginning of a contest. They could even see the twin rudders and propellers as the stern section lifted clear of the water. The bow also reared up to the sky and seemed to wait for timeless seconds.

'No time to break out even one lifeboat,' a lookout breathed.

Kretschmer remained silent.

There was a roar of water cascading into the stricken ship, and the two halves settled lower in the water – a swirl of black water and then nothing – not even wreckage. That would come later as the remains of the ship twisted and turned on their leisurely five-mile glide to the floor of the Atlantic Ocean.

Less than fifty seconds had elapsed between the torpedo explosion and the disappearance of the ship. None of *U99*'s crew had ever known a vessel to sink so quickly.

Chief Petty Officer Jupp Kassel, sitting below at the radio turned to the international distress frequency, with pencil poised to get the ship's name, heard nothing. It was conclusive proof that the magnetic torpedo, with its ability to break a ship's back, and Kretschmer's point-blank range surface attack tactics, made *U99* the most deadly weapon of war in the North Atlantic.

U99's devastating war patrol was over. There was little else she could do now but set course east for the U-boat quays of Lorient.

4

That night, in the lounge of the Hotel Beau Séjour, Sub-Lieutenant Richard Stein was struggling to the top of the unsteady pyramid of armchairs and settees. He warded off the giggling typist's cushion blows and grabbed her around the waist. In accordance with the rules, she submitted to a long, passionate kiss while the cheering U-boatmen chanted the seconds. After ten seconds she was entitled to push Stein off the pyramid. Two Waffen SS officers whom Stein had befriended that day during his first few hours in Lorient were pelting the embracing couple with paper streamers.

Weiner and Anders stood by the buffet table and watched as Stein pinioned the girl's arms and fumbled at her blouse buttons. Her protests were drowned in the general uproar.

'What do you think of our crew?' Weiner asked, splashing more wine into Anders' glass.

'They seem competent enough,' Anders replied. He was watching Stein and wondering how he managed to keep his hair and tie neat and straight while struggling with the girl.

Weiner gestured with his glass. 'Who the devil's. that fellow?'

'His name's Stein. He was on my train this morning.' As Anders answered, he realized how at ease he felt with Weiner. Here, at last, was someone prepared to treat him as an equal.

'Damned gatecrashers,' Weiner muttered into his glass. 'He says he's joining *U99*.'

Weiner gave a short, booming laugh. 'Kretschmer won't have him.'

Anders drained his glass. Normally he would have held onto one drink all evening, but now he was relaxed. He decided to enjoy the wine and savour the easy atmosphere between himself and the older man. 'Why not, kaleu?'

The girl suddenly screamed loudly. Stein had torn her blouse open. She clawed at Stein's face, and in retaliation he slapped her hard across the mouth, then caught hold of her hair and savagely jerked her head back. He used his other hand to tear away her bra. Brinkler, *U700*'s doctor and chief engineer, realized that Stein was going too far and tried to climb the pyramid to stop him, but he was dragged away by the two SS officers.

Weiner put down his glass and stared across the room at the frightened girl. Anders sensed what was coming.

'I'm not having that thug spoiling my party, Anders. Have him thrown out.'

Anders laughed uneasily, hoping that Weiner would treat the matter as a joke. But Weiner's face was deadly serious. One of the SS officers had joined Stein and was tugging at the typist's slip beneath her skirt. It was turning into an ugly scene, and some of the other girls were urging their escorts to intervene.

'For Christ's sake stop him,' Weiner said with quiet anger.

A Mercedes tourer drew up outside the hotel, and the driver jumped out to open the passenger door. Admiral Karl Doenitz stepped out and listened to the sounds of the party. He turned to John Kneller, his flag lieutenant, and smiled.

'There are times, John, when I devoutly wish I was still a U-boat commander.'

Doenitz, the commander-in-chief of the U-boat arm, was a shrewd, sharp-featured Prussian in his early fifties. His prematurely grey hair had led to his U-boat crews giving him the nickname 'The Grey Lion'. Doenitz didn't care. So long as his beloved U-boats sank plenty of ships, they could call him what they liked. After every patrol he would go carefully over the U-boat commander's report word by word and unmercifully castigate any officer who had shown the slightest weakness or hesitation in pressing home an attack. In return, Doenitz fiercely protected his

U-boatmen from the Berlin clique of string-pullers and propagandists. He tolerated a few SS in his headquarters, provided they concerned themselves with security and kept their noses out of U-boat affairs. There were many in Berlin who disliked him. They suspected that his organization of Prien's penetration of Scapa Flow to sink the *Royal Oak* at her anchorage in Scotland had been a stunt to win support from Hitler who had little patience or understanding of U-boat warfare. Goering heartily detested Doenitz because he had been forced to provide Doenitz with a squadron of long-range Kondor aircraft for convoy reconnaissance. Ever since, Goering had ceaselessly but unsuccessfully striven for the return of the Kondors so that his favourite expression 'everything that flies belongs to me' would once again have meaning.

As they entered the hotel, Doenitz said, 'You warned Weiner that I would put in an appearance at his party?'

'Yes, admiral.'

Doenitz didn't want his U-boatmen to feel that he was breathing down their necks even when they were relaxing.

Anders reluctantly put down his glass and pushed through the crowd clustered around the swaying pile of furniture. Stein and the SS officer had removed most of the terrified typist's clothes.

'That's enough, Stein. Leave her alone.'

The crowd fell silent. A restraining hand reached out for Anders' sleeve, but he shrugged it aside. Stein laughed drunkenly and poured the contents of a bottle of wine over the girl's stomach.

'She's enjoying it, Anders. Come and drink from her navel.'

Anders stepped closer and stared up at Stein. His face was level with Stein's gleaming toecap.

'I said that's enough!'

The girl struggled and whimpered as the SS officer started to force her legs apart.

'Try and stop us,' Stein sneered. He lashed out his foot at Anders' face – a move that Anders expected, for Stein found himself kicking at empty air. Then two powerful hands grasped his flailing ankle and twisted viciously. Stein's scream of pain was drowned in the uproar as the rickety pyramid collapsed in a confusion of scattered cushions and flailing arms and legs. There was an outburst of applause from the revellers. As Anders helped the sobbing girl to her feet he saw Doenitz enter the room. There was no mistaking the birdlike features beneath the high-peaked, gold-braided cap.

The dance band conductor had also spotted the admiral's uniform out of the corner of his eye and had launched his musicians into a fast dance number.

Stein failed to see the new arrival. Intent only on revenge, he spun Anders around and hit him unexpectedly in the ribs. It wasn't a hard punch because Stein's SS friends were pulling him away. Two women swooped on the distraught typist and helped her to a door. Brinkler and another member of *U700*'s crew held Anders steady for a few seconds until he had calmed down sufficiently to be allowed to make his way to the buffet where Weiner was pouring Admiral Doenitz a drink. Whitecoated stewards started moving the furniture back into place, and couples resumed dancing.

Weiner clapped Anders genially on the back and introduced him to Doenitz.

Doenitz turned to Anders with an amused smile and nodded to Stein who was scowling at the buffet from across the dance floor. 'Never take your eyes off the enemy for an instant during battle, Anders,' said Doenitz. 'But I like to see a determined attack.'

Anders took the drink Weiner offered and forced

himself to realize he was being addressed by the flag officer of every submarine in the *Kriegsmarine*.

'A momentary lapse, admiral,' Anders said uncertainly. But Doenitz wasn't listening – Kneller was whispering in his ear. The admiral placed his glass on the table, made a hurried apology to Weiner, and followed Kneller to the hotel lobby.

Weiner gloomily watched him leave. 'Well,' he said sadly, 'I suppose a brief visit is better than no visit at all.'

Anders turned and noticed Stein shrug aside the restraining hands of the two SS officers and stand up, his eyes fixed intently in Anders' direction. Somehow, Stein's appearance was still immaculate despite the recent mêlée.

'Trouble approaches,' Weiner said as Stein threaded an unsteady path across the lounge.

But Stein's anger seemed to have vanished. He smiled warmly at Anders. 'I see you're friendly with Uncle Karl,' he said, his speech slurred. 'If I were you, I'd exploit that friendship to get him to transfer you to a decent boat.'

Embarrassed, Anders said, 'This is Captain Hans Weiner – commanding officer of *U700*.'

Stein's smile broadened. He pretended to notice Weiner for the first time.

'Very sorry, kaleu. Just my little joke.'

'A pity to waste it,' Weiner observed coldly. 'Go and see if you can persuade your SS friends to laugh at it.'

Stein bowed mockingly and headed unsteadily back to his table.

'Cocky little bastard,' Weiner growled.

'Captain Weiner?'

Weiner turned. It was Kneller, all teeth and smiles. 'The admiral sends his apologies and regrets that he won't be able to return to the party for at least an hour.'

'Why not?'

'We received a message from the dockyard superintendent requesting permission to switch the Pier Three floodlights on. A U-boat is returning from a war patrol.'

'Which one?' Weiner growled, sensing a threat to his party.

'*U99*,' Kneller said, grinning even more broadly at Weiner's dismayed expression. 'Kretschmer's back.' He stepped on to a chair and clapped his hands for silence. '*U99* is about to enter the harbour,' he announced.

The news triggered a mass exodus.

There were nearly a hundred late-night revellers lined up along both jetties and the quayside that formed Pier Three. Some girls had even climbed on to *U700*'s bridge, and some crowded around the anti-aircraft gun on the raised wintergarten deck. Anders stood on the quayside beside Weiner. Doenitz, in his long greatcoat, was standing near a group of seamen who were ready with a wooden gangway. The only sound was the soft lap of water and the shivering of the less hardy girls in thin party dresses. Stein, his eyes alight with anticipation, stood between his two SS friends. Everyone was watching the navigation lights that were moving across the dark waters of the Scorff Estuary toward the oasis of Pier Three's floodlighting.

There was a film of night mist rising off the still, black water. For some seconds all that could be seen of the U-boat were the glowing navigation lights. Then Anders could discern the dark mass between the lights.

The crowd stirred at the sight of the motionless figure hunched over the bridge coaming. He seemed to be riding through the mist like the avenging spirit of the Rhine.

The shark-like bow slipped with sure precision under the pool of light that bathed the pier. The motors went astern, and the entire length of the secretive creature of the Atlantic night was exposed to view. Anders' attention was riveted on an object that gleamed on the side of the conning tower. It was part of a half-believed legend – something he thought the papers and newsreels had invented. And yet there it was – shining under the floodlights: a golden horseshoe.

'God,' Weiner muttered, craning his bull neck level with Anders' shoulder. 'Look at those pennants.'

A string of homemade flags drooped lifelessly from the periscope standards. Each one represented a ship sunk and was marked with a tonnage figure.

The U-boat's electric motors stopped.

The silence was suddenly broken when a girl began to clap. Another girl joined in. Then another. After a few moments the entire ensemble gathered around Pier Three was applauding and cheering. Even Doenitz joined in, but in keeping with his dignity, he did not cheer. Stein did both with great gusto – his eyes shining with pride as he looked on the boat that he was to join.

Eager, outstretched hands caught the mooring lines that were tossed ashore. *U99* was quickly made fast and the gangway run out to her foredeck. Kretschmer made no attempt to leave his boat until all forty-four members of his crew had filed ashore. He followed a man on a stretcher and shook hands with Doenitz who was waiting at the foot of the gangway.

The man on the stretcher was carried past Anders and Weiner. The blanket covering the wounded man was caked with congealed blood in the region of the man's stomach. It was Anders' first sight of blood drawn by the enemy and a reminder that the U-boats, despite the hysterical claims in the press, were not invincible. He felt a vicelike but reassuring grip on his arm.

'Come on,' Weiner muttered. 'Let's bring the commissioning party back to life.'

*   *   *

Less than 25 couples bothered to return to the party. Stein sat at a table between the two Waffen SS officers and wondered if befriending them had been a mistake. He looked at the group standing near the depleted buffet through a haze of drunken jealousy. Kretschmer, Weiner, Anders, Doenitz, and Weiner's bellowing laugh could be plainly heard above the band that was playing a slow waltz.

'God damn it,' Stein muttered into his beer tankard. 'Should've invited me over. Kretschmer's my CO now . . .'

The dance number came to an end. There was some desultory clapping. Most of the dancers drifted back to their tables. It was now 3:00 A.M.

Stein's hand went to his tie to make sure it was straight. He stood with the intention of walking over to the group but was pulled back onto his chair.

'Don't be a fool,' the SS officer growled.

Kretschmer was passing around a packet of his black cheroots.

Doenitz declined and said warningly to Anders who had accepted one of the cellophane-wrapped cigars:

'Treat it with great respect – they're more dangerous than his torpedoes.'

'Three failures,' Kretschmer said. 'They're getting better.'

Doenitz frowned. He hadn't had an opportunity to go over Kretschmer's war diary of the cruise. He made a brief apology to Weiner and Anders, and took Kretschmer to one side.

'Three failures?'

'Better than the last cruise,' Kretschmer said, 'but they're still not perfect. I lost three ships – one of them a tanker.'

Doenitz muttered an oath. The magnetic torpedo, though a brilliant concept, had been dogged by teething

29

troubles since it had been introduced. So serious had been the failures in the early days that Doenitz once had declared that sailors had never before been sent to war with such a useless weapon. There had even been a court-martialling of the technicians responsible for the torpedo's development. But the German navy's production of a torpedo that didn't sink ships had been balanced by the British production of an anti-submarine bomb that didn't sink submarines, although there were disturbing intelligence reports that the RAF was perfecting an air-borne depth charge.

'At least three failures shows a marked improvement,' Doenitz said, 'but it's still three failures too many.' He paused. 'However, your new second watch officer has recently completed a familiarization course on the G7e warhead at Kiel and knows how to test their depth-keeping chambers before they're fired.'

Kretschmer looked interested. 'What's his name?'

'Sub-Lieutenant Richard Stein. That's him over there.'

Kretschmer's expressionless face studied Stein, who was unaware he was being watched. One of the SS made a joke. All three at the table laughed uproariously. Kretschmer carefully placed his glass down on the buffet and said, 'A small favour, admiral.'

Doenitz looked puzzled. 'Anything, Otto.'

'Find me someone else.'

'Reasons?'

Kretschmer permitted himself a rare ghost of a smile. 'Nothing I could put in writing.'

Stein seemed to sense he was being talked about; he stopped laughing and stared across at the two senior officers.

Doenitz nodded understandingly. '*U700* still isn't back to her full complement. I'll get Kneller to tell Stein in the morning.'

5

It was a cold, blustery, late February day in London as Commander Ian Lancaster Fleming RNVR, one-time journalist and stockbroker and now personal assistant to the Director of Naval Intelligence, studied. the three photographs before him. They were pictures of Germany's three U-boat aces: Otto Kretschmer of *U99*; Gunther Prien of *U47*; and Joachim Schepke of *U100*. He examined the photographs carefully, assimilating every detail of the three faces before him.

Suave, debonair, and frustratingly desk-bound, Fleming had more than a sneaking regard for the three U-boat aces, although he doubted if his regard for these men who were well on their way to sinking one and a half million tons of allied shipping would find much support in the carpeted and carbolic corridors of the admiralty.

The picture of Schepke showed a tall blond man surrounded by an adoring crowd of girls. Kretschmer's unsmiling, sardonic features had been captured by a studio photographer. The picture of the stocky Prien, grinning arrogantly at the camera, had been taken by a CBS News photographer shortly after the U-boat commander's destruction of the British battleship *Royal Oak* at its supposedly safe Scapa Flow anchorage in Scotland.

Fleming read an intelligence report on the three men and sighed: a character in a novel who was a combination of the swashbuckling Schepke, the arrogant Prien, and the ruthless, calculating Kretschmer would make an ideal hero in every respect.

Fleming pushed the photographs to the corner of his

desk and weighted them with a fragment of forged steel. The curved surface of the makeshift paperweight gleamed black and forbidding. He regarded it thoughtfully for a few moments before summoning a stenographer. He dictated rapidly to her for ten minutes.

The words came easily.

Admiral Godfrey, the Director of Naval Intelligence, read Fleming's report before the others because he knew it would be lively and spiced with picturesque phrases, a welcome change from the reams of turgid civil service prose that landed on his desk each day.

He read through the report once for enjoyment (he particularly liked the neat description of the three U-boat aces as 'the blunt instrument of Doenitz's carefully evolved U-boat strategy') and a second time to consider the implications of its conclusions. As was usual with Fleming's schemes, it was outlandish and imaginative but not impractical, although it did venture into the politically sensitive area that involved the neutral United States.

Fleming's closing words were, 'If we mice do manage, by some miracle, to catch ourselves a pussy cat, we ought to invite our cousins over to take a close look at its teeth and claws in exchange for some of their cheese.'

Admiral Godfrey chuckled to himself and scribbled 'agreed' at the foot of the page. He then sat back and read through the report for a third time.

Ian Fleming, he thought to himself, was an extraordinarily entertaining writer.

6

It was the morning after *U700*'s commissioning party.

Stein's face was a mask of unbridled fury as he stood rigidly at attention on the quayside at Lorient. With the other members of *U700*'s crew, he kept his arm and hand at the correct angle for the salute while the army band played the German national anthem. A rain-sodden sheet of music was snatched from a flute player by the biting East wind and wrapped around Stein's trouser leg, yet one more humiliation in a series that had started the previous evening and had culminated with him having to stand beside Anders and Weiner and the other members of *U700*'s crew.

The band finished playing, and Doenitz stepped forward to face *U700*'s officers and men. He cleared his throat and delivered a short, simple speech, expounding his favourite theme of the need for U-boats to press home the attack relentlessly when engaging a convoy.

Stein paid little attention, allowing his gaze to wander to the battle-scarred *U99* lying alongside *U700*. Kretschmer was standing on the veteran U-boat's deck casing in earnest conversation with his first watch officer. Stein wondered what the two men were talking about – probably discussing *U99*'s battle tactics on her next war patrol. His scowl deepened.

Doenitz finished his speech. Weiner stepped forward to accept *U700*'s logbook and pennant from the admiral, thanked him, and stepped back.

The simple ceremony was over; *U700* was now a fully commissioned, frontline U-boat. After the two shakedown cruises necessary to weld her crew into one close-knit fighting team, she would be ready for the bitter war being fought in the Atlantic.

7

Weiner tapped his pointer on the wall chart, described a circle around Iceland, and then turned his stocky frame to face *U700*'s crew. Anders sat in the front row, his long, loose-limbed legs stretched out across the polished floor. Apart from Stein's brooding presence, the atmosphere was relaxed and friendly. Stein was sitting alone at a window, gazing down at *U99*. The seasoned U-boat had been hastily refitted and repainted and now matched *U700* for smartness.

'I can't tell you our exact patrol position,' Weiner said, his rich voice booming in the large room, 'but I can tell you that it will be within range of RAF Coastal Command Catalinas and Hudsons operating from Iceland. Standing orders require four bridge lookouts and a continuous sky periscope watch. Remember, gentlemen – the aircraft is the U-boat's most mortal enemy.'

A band outside started playing the *Kretschmer March*, a piece specially composed by the bandmaster in honour of *U99*'s commander. Weiner noticed that Stein was tapping an immaculately polished shoe in time with the music. Two engine-room petty officers edged nearer the window and glanced down at the scene below. Members of a farewell party were waving to *U99* as it cast off.

'Shall we concentrate on *U700*, gentlemen?' Weiner asked, grinning wolfishly. 'I'm sure *U99* can look after herself.'

There was polite laughter. Weiner smiled and lifted into place a large picture that showed a torpedo exploding against the side of a ship.

'A conventional torpedo warhead detonates when its firing pistol strikes the side of a ship's hull – half the explosive force goes into the air doing no harm, and moreover, the side of the ship where the explosion takes place tells the convoy escort where the U-boat is to be found.'

Weiner lifted another picture into position. 'This, gentlemen, is what a magnetic warhead can do.'

Anders studied the picture with interest. It showed a torpedo exploding directly beneath a ship's keel. Weiner leaned on his pointer.

'You will be pleased to know that *U99* has been using the new version of the magnetic warhead and reports vastly improved reliability. As you can see, the explosive force, instead of going into the air as it does with a conventional warhead, is concentrated wholly on the ship's keel. And with the new Wotan steel used to encase the warhead to double the explosive force, one torpedo is sufficient to break a twenty-thousand tonner's back in two.'

Weiner had the attention of everyone in the room with the exception of Stein. 'Another advantage, gentlemen, is the lack of flash when the torpedo explodes. We know that *U47* was able to escape from Scapa Flow after sinking the *Royal Oak* because the British at first thought there had been an explosion in one of their precious battleship's magazines.

'You will also be pleased to know that *U700* has been supplied with one of the new warheads for her first patrol. By the time we leave for our second patrol, I'm sure there will be ample supplies for all fourteen torpedoes to be fitted with magnetic warheads. And that will enable us to adopt Lieutenant-Commander Kretschmer's favourite axiom.'

Weiner broke off and smiled frostily in Stein's direction. 'We are fortunate in having Sub-Lieutenant Richard Stein with us,' he continued. 'Not only has he completed a familiarization course on the new warhead, but he has also made a close study of *U99*'s battle tactics. Perhaps he would be kind enough to advise us of Lieutenant-Commander Kretschmer's axiom regarding the firing of torpedoes.'

Stein turned from the window and met Weiner's freezing smile with an innocent expression.

'Yes, kaleu?' he inquired politely.

Weiner's smile did not desert him.

'You know which axiom I am referring to?'

'Yes, kaleu.'

Weiner maintained the smile with some effort.

'We would like to hear it please, Mr Stein.'

'From whom, captain?'

Someone at the back of the room giggled.

'From you, lieutenant.'

Stein looked blank. 'When, captain?'

This time no one made a sound. Weiner took a pace toward Stein and stared down into the expressionless eyes. Yes, he thought, you'd like that wouldn't you? You'd like me to lose my temper in front of the entire crew.

'Stand up please, Mr Stein,' he said calmly.

Stein stood and made a minor adjustment to his tie.

'Don't worry about your tie, Mr Stein. As usual, your turnout is an example for us all. Please tell us now in a clear voice what *U99*'s battle tactics are regarding the economic expenditure of torpedoes.'

Stein gave a slow, deliberate smile. 'One ship,' he said, and paused for effect. *'One torpedo.'*

8

'One ship, one torpedo,' said Fleming gloomily. He tossed a file across his desk to Brice. 'Here's another – the *Convallaria* – sunk by one torpedo. And another – the *Beatus* – went down in less than a minute. Fifty ships altogether, and all sunk by one blasted torpedo each.'

Alan Brice read through the survivors' account. He was a careful man from the style of his dress to his unhurried Bostonian speech. As a scientist, one of the United States Navy's top torpedo designers, Brice was a disappointment to Fleming, who preferred his scientists to have characteristics that identified them as such: an eccentric nature, hair standing on end, egg on tie, and maybe a beautiful daughter thrown in for luck. The tall, blond American in his neat suit looked more like a product of Harvard than MIT. But he did have a beautiful daughter – he had shown Fleming her photograph – who was three.

Fleming cleared his throat.

'One thing all those reports have in common, Mr Brice, the survivors of nearly every ship talk about one explosion from *beneath* the ship, not the side. Also convoy escorts are complaining that there's no flash from the explosions to tell them where the U-boat's lurking. If your Newport Torpedo Station wants proof that the Germans have perfected the magnetic warhead idea, there it is.'

Brice returned the reports to Fleming's desk.

'It sure looks that way, commander. But I understand you're still losing ships by the old method – a fan of four contact torpedoes fired at one ship in daylight.'

Fleming smiled. Despite his measured speech, Brice was

37

no fool. 'We suspect that the new warheads are not yet in full production – that aces such as Kretschmer get priority.'

'The man with the golden horseshoe?'

You have done your homework, Fleming thought. He said, 'Kretschmer specializes in the surface night attack. He's been seen often enough – charging up and down the convoy lines, shooting his torpedoes at point-blank range.' Fleming's tone became morose. 'We think the wretched fellow's forgotten he's driving a submarine.'

'But it still needs one helluva bang for one torpedo to sink a ship – even a torpedo fitted with a magnetic warhead,' Brice said.

Fleming indicated a piece of metal that served as a paperweight. 'That and several other pieces of the same type of steel were found embedded in what was left of the *Royal Oak*'s keel after Prien had finished with her. It's a new type of Krupps Wotan armour with a tensile strength of one hundred tons per square inch. Our boffins – scientists,' Fleming quickly amended, seeing Brice's puzzled expression, 'are laying even money that Jerry's using his new steel to encase the magnetic warheads.'

Brice turned the piece of metal over in his fingers. 'I should say that that's a reasonably safe bet, commander. Is this a preliminary offer in exchange for information on our development work on torpedoes?'

Fleming smiled. He decided that he was going to enjoy dealing with the blond American. 'Consider it a down payment, old boy.'

Brice replaced the metal fragment on Fleming's desk. 'I suspect that my Admiral Swaffer will want something more substantial than this before he agrees to pooling information.'

Suddenly Fleming was serious. 'A general order has been issued which gives the capture of an *intact* German U-boat a number one priority. You tell your Admiral

Swaffer that we might be able to give you the chance of a close look at a Wotan warhead sooner than you think.'

After Brice had gone Fleming picked up the first of two reports that the pretty Wren writer had dropped in his tray. According to an observant Breton agent in Lorient, *U47*, *U100*, and *U99* had sailed that week. For the first time, the three aces – Prien, Schepke, and Kretschmer – were on patrol together.

The second report was more interesting. It confirmed that the new radar device fitted to a destroyer in one of the newly formed escort groups under the command of HMS *Walker* had been tested and found satisfactory. What little Fleming knew about precision radar was enough to convince him that it held the key to the eventual destruction of the U-boats. It was not the clumsy longwave equipment that the Germans had, but radio ranging using very short frequencies that yielded crisp echoes, which could be accurately plotted on a screen.

Fleming opened his private file on the three U-boat aces. Kretschmer's photograph was on top, and he gazed down at the handsome, unsmiling features.

'Soon, you bastard,' Fleming murmured to himself. 'Soon.'

9

At three minutes past midnight on February 26, 1941, U-boat operations room at Lorient received a signal from *U47* commanded by Gunther Prien saying that he had sighted a large convoy heading east.

Doenitz moved from his chair with its commanding view

of the giant plot table of the North Atlantic and beckoned to the operations room duty officer.

Five minutes later a signal was sent to Prien ordering him to shadow the convoy and send frequent reports on its course and speed so that other U-boats could be directed to the convoy for a mass surface attack. It was a technique that had been used with astonishing success against Convoy SC7 the previous October; of the 35 ships that left Nova Scotia, only half survived the U-boats to reach Liverpool. The surface night attack was Doenitz's own concept, based on his experiences as a U-boat commander during the Great War when he had discovered that the low profile of a surfaced U-boat was virtually impossible for the enemy to see no matter what detection equipment he used. Before the war Doenitz had even published a book, in which he had outlined the principles of the future of U-boat warfare. So far, those principles had been proved right; the Royal Navy's prized Asdic submarine detection equipment had proved virtually useless against a surfaced U-boat, and his commanders were learning not to fear it. And even if a U-boat was detected, it was not unknown for the commander to surface contemptuously within sight of an escorting sloop or corvette and use its superior surface speed to make an escape.

Kneller interrupted Doenitz's thoughts. '*U47* has been forced to break off shadowing, admiral.'

Doenitz's thin eyebrows went up. The stocky Prien, one of the few U-boat commanders who was a party member, was not the sort of man to give up; he would cling tenaciously to the convoy until ordered to attack.

'Did he say why?'

'He says that he was driven off by a destroyer that came straight at him,' Kneller replied.

'At night?' Doenitz asked incredulously.

Thirty minutes later Prien re-established contact with

the convoy but was again driven off by a 'destroyer that came straight at me.'

Prien was ordered to regain contact but was driven off for the third time. This time he managed to get the destroyer's number. OKM intelligence identified the warship as HMS *Walker*.

'It's as if the British can see in the dark,' was Kneller's gloomy comment on the night's proceedings.

Doenitz went to bed at 3:00 A.M. Kneller's comment triggered a nagging worry that kept him awake until dawn.

10

U700's first shakedown cruise was turning into a disaster. For the third time that day Bernard Anders jabbed a bony finger on the Klaxon button and screamed, 'Diving stations! Aircraft!' This time he had to bellow at the fumbling gun crew, 'Come on! Move!'

The diesel exhaust vent spewed a sudden cloud of black smoke. The Krupp steel beneath Anders' feet began pounding in harmony with the two MAN diesels as they opened up to full power. The gun crew centred the main gun and raced along the casing to the bridge. Below in the control room, Stein started his stopwatch at the exact moment the sirens started howling. Brinkler was roundly cursing his petty officer coxswain for being a fraction of a second late in spinning the hydroplane wheel. A lookout lost his footing on the ladder and tumbled into the control room. He sat on the floor dazed.

'Out! Out!' Stein screamed. He grabbed the lookout by the scruff of the neck and virtually threw him through the circular door that led aft. A sudden tangle of arms and legs in the control room caused by lookouts not moving out of the way quickly enough could spell disaster for a crash-diving submarine.

U700 tilted down as Anders followed the gun crew down the ladder. The boat was being driven under by the superior power of the diesels; Brinkler would wait until the last second before the hatches closed to switch over to the less powerful electric motors. Water was roaring into the ballast tanks as Anders reached up and slammed the hatch shut and spun the handwheel. He was about to shout down to the control room that the hatch was secure when there was a sudden explosion in his ears. It felt as if his skull had been blown apart. He gave a cry and tumbled through the attack kiosk into the control room. It was some seconds before he could hear the commotion around him – Brinkler was obviously in pain too as he roundly cursed the hydroplane coxswain for being too slow.

'Ears,' Stein mumbled, hanging onto a pipe and moving his hair-cream slicked head from side to side.

Anders climbed shakily to his feet. He forgot his lanky frame and struck his head on a manometer pipe. Weiner had disappeared, but his powerful voice could be heard from aft bellowing angrily. Moments later he propelled his bulk into the control room and looked at Anders and Stein in concern.

'Are you two all right?'

Anders, determined not to show weakness in front of his commanding officer, had come to attention. Stein had done the same and had given Anders the satisfaction of seeing a lock of hair fall out of place.

'Yes, kaleu,' Anders responded promptly.

'Damned diesel machinist didn't shut the engines off in time,' Weiner growled, his eyes fixed on the overhead depth gauge pointers that were edging down to the forty metre mark.

The two fifteen-hundred-horsepower diesels had been allowed to continue running for a fraction of a second after the hatches had been closed with the consequence that virtually all the air in the boat had been sucked into their cylinders.

'Forty metres,' Brinkler called out.

Stein's thumb automatically stopped the clicking stop-watch.

'Well?' Weiner demanded.

Stein pushed the offending lock of hair into place. 'One minute twenty, kaleu.'

Weiner muttered an oath under his breath. Anders could understand how he felt. The time to reach the required forty metres depth had taken twelve seconds more than the last dive.

Weiner leaned against the commander's chart table. 'Know how quickly Kretschmer can take *U99* down, Anders?'

Stein opened his mouth to answer.

'I'm asking Anders,' Weiner said curtly.

Stein closed his mouth and smiled sourly at Anders.

Suddenly the figure Anders knew by heart wasn't there.

'Well?' Weiner prompted.

'I'm sorry, kaleu,' Anders said, desperately searching his memory.

'Stein?'

'Thirty seconds,' Stein said smugly.

Weiner nodded. 'Thirty seconds,' he repeated sadly. 'And *U700* won't be allowed on patrol until she can get into the cellar in less than sixty seconds on ten successive dives. Did you know that, Anders?'

Anders shook his head. 'No, kaleu.' He avoided his commanding officer's eyes. He felt that he had failed Weiner – that *U700*'s poor performance was entirely his fault.

Weiner said nothing, sensing that Anders was assuming

43

responsibility for the U-boat's appalling showing. He was tempted to reassure Anders but decided against it. Goddamn it, he was Anders' commanding officer – not his father. If Anders felt he was to blame, that was his problem.

'Let's try again,' Weiner growled. 'Stand by to surface.' He swung up the ladder into the attack kiosk and sat at the periscope. As he watched the strengthening green light from the sun filtering down from the surface, he knew that his greatest problem was going to be Anders' lack of confidence and Stein's overconfidence.

He wondered how long it would be before *U700* would be ready for sea and whether there would be any enemy ships left for his U-boat when it was ready.

Kretschmer, Schepke, and Prien had already sunk well over a million tons between them.

11

On March 10, the British got their revenge on Prien for the *Royal Oak* and the 786 officers and men who perished with it.

Doenitz sat in his chair in the Lorient U-boat operations room for twelve hours, gazing down at U47's marker on a giant plot table. Waiting.

The cipher clerk set her machine to 'transmit' and tapped out for the tenth time that hour, '*DBU to U47. Report your position.*'

She set her machine to 'receive' and sat back. The keyboard remained silent.

Kneller set a cup of coffee down before his admiral but Doenitz allowed it to get cold. He found it impossible to believe that the British had finally caught up with the bumptious but cunning Nazi. Although Prien was probably the most heartily disliked commander in the U-boat arm, he was nevertheless a courageous officer and would be sorely missed.

There was worse to come, for during that March of 1941 the British escort group headed by HMS *Walker* had put to sea. They were the first submarine hunter-killer group to be equipped with what was later to prove the most decisive weapon in the struggle that Winston Churchill termed 'The Battle of the Atlantic'.

That weapon was radar.

12

March 17, St Patrick's Day, was ten minutes old when Patrick Gallagher left Toomley's pub through the open saloon window because it looked as if the fight was going to get out of hand. After the British, violence was Gallagher's biggest hate and the opening rumbles of a dispute, especially disputes in pubs, were the signal for him to head for the horizon. Ever since he had seen as a boy the despised Black and Tans at work in Dublin during the Troubles, violence of any kind had revolted him. His many friends and fellow telegraphers who manned the Valentia Bay trans-Atlantic cable station mistakenly considered Gallagher a coward. Rather than have to prove them wrong, Gallagher found it easier to agree with them cheerfully.

A cold wind was blowing in from the Atlantic across the bay. He pulled his collar up, crossed the road, and stood for some moments, drawing on a cigarette and listening to the sea fretting at the rocks. It would be a good night for a spot of sea fishing. There was a big conger eel he was after.

The sound of breaking glass from the bar broke in on his thoughts. A door burst open, spilling light and foul language into the night. It would be only a matter of time before the police arrived. Gallagher walked to his motorcycle. The machine and fishing were the only loves in his lonely life. He looked at the bike with pride. It was a magnificent flat-twin Douglas with an Ulster registration. As usual, the finely turned machine started on the first kick. A truck loaded to the roof with police screeched to a standstill outside the pub just as he was easing the machine on to the road. He was a hundred yards away and accelerating hard by the time the uniformed lads were making their first 1941 St Patrick's Day arrests. The icy wind wrenched his amiable features into a tight grimace.

Only when he was a comfortable mile from Toomley's pub did he ease up to the throttle. He was paid to stay out of trouble. And with the exchange rate of the German mark against the pound being what it was, he was paid very well indeed. He began humming a tune that he had learned from his German friends during his motorcycle fishing trips to the Black Forest in the late 1930s. He couldn't remember the original German words but the translated lyric was pleasant enough: *We're marching to war against England!*

13

While Patrick Gallagher was riding home, some 500 miles out in the Atlantic, Commander Joachim Schepke of *U100* and second to Kretschmer in the tonnage sunk league was dying a particularly unpleasant death. His U-boat had just been rammed by a destroyer that had come straight at him from out of the darkness as if the British, by some uncanny instinct, knew exactly where to find him. Schepke had stared in fascination at the destroyer's shuddering bow as it drove toward him like a charging cliff. He was confident that *U100* hadn't been seen, that the warship was racing to the aid of a glowing tanker on the horizon that Kretschmer had torpedoed half an hour previously. For a moment it had seemed that the destroyer would miss the stern of *U100* by centimetres. But at the last moment the monstrous bow made a sudden change of direction. The warning Schepke had been about to scream down the bridge voice pipe died on his lips. He stared aghast at the pounding, 30,000 horsepower apparition that was thundering straight at him behind a huge curtain of spray. He was unable to shout – unable to make the slightest move to save his life. There was a scream of metal on metal as the knife-edge bow sliced into the bridge coaming. Schepke was hurled against the torpedo aimer and felt a strange numbness in his legs. He lashed out in panic and grabbed hold of the attack periscope. There was a curious lightness in his body as he fought to prevent himself from going under, dimly aware of the destroyer's towering, flat-sided hull racing past. Something at the back of his reeling mind warned him about the danger from the warship's churning propellers. He clung desperately to the periscope standard that was now lying almost flat on the surface, or whatever it was he could judge was the surface in that seething maelstrom. It was when he tried to fend his body away from the British warship's rust-streaked side with his feet that he realized why it was that his body felt so light. His legs had been severed from his torso; there was nothing left to his body from the waist down.

U100 was sinking beneath him, dragging him down.

All he had to do was release his grip on the periscope standard and his oddly truncated body would bob to the surface.

But suddenly there didn't seem to be much point in letting go.

Kretschmer was unaware of Schepke's fate. He had expended all his torpedoes and sunk a total of five ships during the night's action. The remains of three targets were burning brightly in the distance. They had been a U-boat commander's most prized victims: tankers.

There was now nothing to do but set a course for Lorient, hand over to his first watch officer, and dine on coffee and sandwiches.

But the radar-equipped destroyer in HMS *Walker*'s hunter-killer escort group had detected *U99*'s presence on surface and was closing in fast on the unsuspecting U-boat.

14

At the exact moment that the pulverized remains of Kretschmer's *U99* sank for the last time, a light drizzle began to fall on Lorient, splattering against the blackout windows of the U-boat operations room.

Doenitz was sitting in his usual chair beside Kneller, saying nothing. Weiner, Anders, and Stein were in the gallery overlooking the giant map of the North Atlantic. *U700* had completed its shakedown cruise and had returned to Lorient. Doenitz liked his officers to familiarize themselves with the behind-the-scenes procedures, and the three men were sitting very still, leaning forward to catch the whispered exchanges between the controller and Doenitz.

A girl added the name of the *J B White* to the wall-mounted blackboard. It was the last ship to have been claimed as sunk that night. Her chalk squeaked noisily in the hushed room. An assistant flipped through Lloyd's and called out the *J B White*'s tonnage.

The cipher clerk stared down at the printing head of her silent machine. She had spent the last hour broadcasting repeated requests to *U99* and *U100* to report their positions. Each time, the reply from the Atlantic had been silence.

Anders touched Stein's sleeve and whispered, 'Maybe they've dived and can't use their radio.'

Stein shook his immaculate head. 'Kretschmer would never dive during an action. Nor would Schepke. You've read their standing orders to their crews: "Always remain on surface unless in dire peril."'

Anders fell silent. What Stein said made sense; a U-boat was essentially a craft designed to spend most of its time on the surface with the ability to dive to initiate a daylight attack or escape an air attack. Many U-boats were now returning from patrol without having dived once; a submerged U-boat under attack was a helpless U-boat, wholly dependent on the evasion skills of its captain.

The sudden click of the cipher machine interrupted Anders' thoughts. It was a noise he had come to recognize as the mechanical equivalent of a clearing of the throat. The cipher clerk and everyone else in the room looked expectantly at the machine. Its printing head rattled briefly across the paper and stopped. The girl tore the flimsy off the roll and passed it to an assistant who in turn handed it to the controller. He read it and looked across at Doenitz's sharp, inquiring features.

'It's from *U37*, admiral. She reports having broken off

the attack and has been unable to contact *U99* and *U100*.'

Anders met Weiner's eye and guessed what the admiral was thinking: first Prien a few days ago and now Schepke and Kretschmer in one night. It just didn't seem possible. And if the enemy could sweep such U-boats from the board, what of *U700* and her inexperienced crew?

Two long cues reached across the plot table and moved the markers for *U99* and *U100* to the 'overdue reporting' square at the edge of the plot. If nothing was heard from the U-boats for seventy-two hours the markers would be removed and Admiral Doenitz would have the task of signing letters to relatives that began: 'It is with deepest regret that I have to inform you . . .'

As Anders stared down at the giant map, it occurred to him that the plot table resembled a grotesque board game, a game with no rules, a game with an occasional victor – but many, many losers.

Stein remained seated as Weiner and Anders stood. He was gazing fixedly at the marker for *U99*. Anders touched his shoulder gently.

'It's late. We've got gunnery practice tomorrow.'

Stein nodded and rose to his feet. He gave one last look at the marker with its tiny, inverted golden horseshoe and then, by curious coincidence, said virtually the same thing as a British seaman on HMS *Walker* had said that night as *U99*, bathed in the beam of the destroyer's searchlight, had disappeared from view:

'His horseshoes were upside down. His luck was bound to run out.'

15

The sun was shining in London the next day, and Commander Ian Fleming was in a buoyant mood as he and Brice lunched at Scott's.

'I smell good news,' Brice said when the waiter had departed with their order.

'The best news ever,' Fleming said cheerfully. 'We sank two U-boats last night. And not just any old U-boats, but *U99* and *U100*. What do you think of that?'

'A capture would be good news,' Brice said pointedly.

Fleming looked crestfallen. 'I thought you'd be happy for us, Mr Brice. With Prien blown to glory a few days ago, that means our friends have lost their three aces in under a week. It ought to knock a hole in their morale that you could drive a bus through.'

'How did it happen?'

'Schepke's boat was rammed, and Kretschmer was forced to the surface. Unfortunately there was time for a member of his crew to set the scuttling charges. They blew the bottom out of *U99* and it went down like a brick.'

Brice smiled faintly. 'A pity, commander.'

'Please, old boy, call me Ian. *Walker*'s skipper had a boat lowered in the hope of getting a boarding party on to the U-boat, but it was too late. There was similar business in 1939 after *U39* loosed off a couple of torpedoes at the *Ark Royal*. Jerry would sooner scuttle before all the crew are safe than allow a ship to fall into enemy hands. They scuttled their entire grand fleet after the last war in accordance with their rigid tradition of never allowing the enemy to set foot on their warships.'

'Which is not going to make capturing an intact U-boat a . . .' Brice groped for an English expression, '. . . a cup of tea. Right, Ian?'

Fleming smiled. 'We live in hope, old boy.'

'In the meantime, I have to live nearly four thousand miles from my family.'

'You're not getting bored with London are you?' Fleming asked, looking mildly shocked.

'Frankly, yes. And don't go quoting Samuel Johnson at me.'

The waiter returned with their soup. Fleming tasted it cautiously and murmured when the waiter had gone, 'At least they're trying. How about a nice young lady to show you the sights? There's a suitable one in my address book.'

'I'll have you know that I'm a happily married man,' Brice said indignantly.

'You needn't worry about Clare,' Fleming said drily. 'She's a very proper young woman. I've never got anywhere with her, and I'm available.'

Brice laughed at Fleming's dead-pan expression.

16

Seven weeks later, on May 9, 1941, the British succeeded in capturing *U110*, commanded by Fritz Lemp, the man who, on the first day of the war, had mistaken the liner *Athenia* for a troopship and had torpedoed it in violation of the then prevailing Prize Ordinance Regulations.

The circumstances of the capture were kept a secret because the British didn't want to alert the Germans to the fact that they were intent on capturing a U-boat. Lemp's periscope had been spotted shortly after he had carried out a conventional submerged daylight attack against the lead ship in a westward bound convoy. Trapped in the escorts' Asdic beams and repeatedly pounded by accurate depth charge patterns, Lemp was forced to blow his tanks and surface.

HMS *Bulldog* was about to ram when the officer commanding the escort group decided that it might be worth trying to implement the admiralty order that urged the capture of an intact U-boat 'if humanly possible'. A boarding party from *Bulldog* succeeded in recovering a good deal of material from the U-boat including an Enigma cipher machine. But the boat was leaking badly, and they were unable to remove the one remaining magnetic torpedo. An attempt was made to tow the U-boat to Iceland, but the *Bulldog* was forced to slip the tow as the U-boat sank deeper in the water. That afternoon, watched by the disappointed boarding party now safely back on the *Bulldog*, *U110* rolled over and sank.

Fleming read Captain Baker-Cresswell's report on May 25 and decided that there was nothing to be gained in telling Brice about the failure.

A pity Lemp had drowned – it would have been interesting to find out exactly why he thought that the *Athenia* had been a troopship.

Fleming initialled the report and tossed it in his out tray.

At least it was one U-boat less.

17

On August 23, 1941, after 18 weeks of intensive training, *U700* went to war.

Weiner's booming voice gave the order to cast off from

Pier Three at precisely twelve noon. He experienced a sensation of foreboding as he stared down from the bridge at the two lines of smartly turned-out men standing on the casing to take the salute.

Men? Dear God, they were little more than boys; nourished, loved and cared for by their parents for nineteen years each, for that was their average age. They had their entire lives to look forward to, and yet here they were riding an iron coffin as *wabo*, or 'depth charge fodder', for an Austrian corporal who cared as much for U-boatmen as he did for their type of warfare, which was little enough.

Weiner watched Anders out of the corner of his eye. The lean, awkward frame of the young officer was bent over the voice pipe issuing orders to the motor room. At least he no longer sought Weiner's confirmation of every course alteration. Three successful patrols by *U700* ought to see Anders with his own command.

A pretty girl detached herself from the small farewell crowd gathered on the quayside and trotted along the wharf to keep pace with the grey U-boat, waving to the impassive crew. Weiner recognized her as the HQ typist who had married boatsman's mate Bruch the week before. Bruch was standing near the main gun, staring straight ahead, feet the regulation distance apart, hands clasped firmly behind his back.

Wave to her, you idiot! Weiner willed. But the long weeks of training had left their mark – Bruch gave no sign that he had seen his bride. The girl stopped and lifted a handkerchief to her eyes as she stared after the departing U-boat.

It was the image of that lonely girl that hardened Weiner's resolve: he would bring *all* his crew back safely at the end of each patrol. He would sink enemy ships by tackling every one that presented itself as a likely target, but he'd make damn certain that the odds were a hundred and ten per cent in his favour first. He'd probably end up sinking more ships than the so-called aces and survive into the bargain. The decision helped to ease the recurring nightmare that had plagued him ever since *U700*'s accident on her trials.

He inhaled deeply. It was a beautiful summer's day. The shrill voices of the Breton fishwives cleaning the morning's catch carried clearly across the Scorff estuary. Anders was allowing the current to swing the U-boat's bows toward the sea. Weiner knew how much Anders enjoyed handling the boat and decided to leave him alone.

'Anders.'

'Yes, kaleu?'

'Take over, please. Dismiss the deck party and call me when the Isle de Groix is on our quarter.'

Anders saluted smartly and ordered the crew below.

'And Anders.'

'Yes, kaleu?'

Weiner pointed a stubby finger at the U-boat's bow. 'That jumping wire was damaged when the torpedoes were struck down. Have it repaired at the first opportunity.'

'I had noticed it, kaleu. One of the boatsman's mates is good at splicing wire. I've told him to carry out repairs on his next watch.'

Weiner gave a satisfied grunt and swung down the ladder leaving Anders alone on the bridge.

Anders opened the watertight box that contained the portable signal lamp and exchanged recognition signals with the minesweeper that was to escort *U700* clear of the estuary. He returned the lamp to its box and flipped open the voice pipe cover.

'Bridge – control room.'

'Control room,' Brinkler's voice answered.

'Bridge lookout party on the double, please.'

Anders then ordered a changeover from the electric

motors to the diesels before closing the voice pipe cover. The four lookouts emerged from the control room and took their positions while Anders hunched over the spray deflector and watched the white water surging past *U700*'s bulging saddle tanks. He felt confident of his ability to handle anything.

Twenty minutes later *U700* was clear of the French fishing harbour and was lifting its raked bow to the long, easy swell of the Atlantic Ocean.

18

Even as Anders yelled 'Aircraft!' and started the siren, Brinkler was flooding the tanks and roaring at his coxswain to spin the hydroplanes down for the fastest crash dive in *U700*'s short history.

One of the lookouts, who by now knew about Brinkler's dives, dropped Anders' binoculars, entangling the strap around the bridge hatch.

'It doesn't matter!' Anders shouted. He yanked the binoculars free and tossed them over the side. The forward deck casing was already awash and a huge wake was creaming past the main gun. Another ten seconds and tons of green Atlantic would be cascading down the U-boat's open hatch.

'For God's sake *move!*' Anders yelled at the last lookout who was half way through the hatch, groping for the ladder with his feet.

The amphibious biplane was less than two kilometres away, but the danger it represented was nothing compared with the danger of Brinkler taking *U700* down with the bridge hatch open. Cursing more in anger than fear,

Anders crashed his boot on the lookout's shoulder and shoved. Then he scrambled down after him and managed to slam the hatch shut just as the bridge was flooded, but too late to avoid being drenched by several litres of icy seawater.

Weiner was trying not to smile as Anders' undignified tangle of arms and legs tumbled angrily into the control room.

'What was it?' he inquired politely.

Anders' pale features were even paler as he climbed to his feet. 'Chief!' he snapped at Brinkler who was levelling out the boat at sixty metres. 'In future you will await confirmation that the hatches are closed and clipped before diving! Is that understood?'

Both Brinkler and Weiner were surprised at Anders' outburst.

You're learning, thought Weiner. There was nothing like a bad fright to put a man on his mettle.

'What was the time taken to get down?' Weiner asked.

'Twenty-nine seconds,' Brinkler answered, keeping his eyes firmly on his gauges.

Weiner nodded his bullet-like head. 'Pretty good, eh, Mr Anders?'

'Yes, kaleu. But the chief . . .'

Brinkler turned in his seat and adopted an injured expression. 'Mr Anders sounded the alarm and yelled "aircraft". From the way he yelled, I thought an entire squadron of Spitfires were on our tail. I decided not to waste time. I naturally thought that the bridge lookout wouldn't waste time either.'

'I'll enter it in the control room log,' said Anders, his face still white with anger.

'Enter the sighting,' Weiner suggested, smiling at the two antagonists. 'And that you dived in twenty-nine seconds.'

Annoyed at Weiner's refusal to discipline Brinkler, Anders turned on his commanding officer. 'There were four lookouts on the bridge plus myself, kaleu. We're not genies that can turn into a puff of smoke and vanish down the hatch whenever the chief decides to take the boat down like an elevator.'

'Let's discuss this in the wardroom,' Weiner said, moving aft. Anders and Brinkler followed him through the water-tight door.

'Now then,' Weiner said, dropping onto the settee-berth. 'As far as I'm concerned you're both in the wrong for arguing in front of the crew.'

'*I* was not arguing with the chief,' Anders protested. 'The chief was arguing with me. He failed . . .'

Weiner held up a cautionary hand. 'He failed to do what, Mr Anders? He got the boat down in less than thirty seconds – the minimum possible time. So if anything, you were late in getting the hatch shut.'

Anders opened his mouth, but Weiner cut him short and turned to Brinkler. 'In future, chief, you will wait until you receive confirmation that the hatches are shut and clipped before taking the boat down.' Weiner regarded his first officer steadily. 'And you, Mr Anders, will train your lookouts to move faster. Now that's settled, and we're away from the weather. I trust you gentlemen will join me in a brandy after your watch.'

19

'What do you think you're doing in here, Helmann?' Anders demanded irritably.

The torpedoman, a nervous 19-year-old, hesitated, one

leg through the watertight door that led into the control room. His eyes were round and worried.

'Well?' Anders snapped.

Helmann mumbled an apology and withdrew, moving back to the safety of the bow torpedo room. He paused on the companionway outside the second officer's berth. Sub-Lieutenant Stein had rigged up a blanket as a curtain and Helmann could see the glow of a reading lamp through the thin material. Helmann was undecided. To him, petty officers were tyrants, and officers were worse. Suddenly the curtain whipped back.

'Yes?'

The low reading light caught Stein's sabre scar at a frightening angle. The youngster would have turned and fled, but Stein caught hold of his arm.

'Helmann isn't it? What's the matter?'

Helmann swallowed and tried to back away. 'Nothing, Mr Stein,' he stammered.

'Then why were you standing there like that? Planning something were you?'

Helmann bit his lower lip. 'It's Bruch, Mr Stein. I can't find him.'

Stein remembered that Helmann had been the best man at Bruch's wedding a few days before *U700* had sailed.

'Have you checked aft? If he's off watch he might be with those chess maniacs in the motor room.'

'I don't like to go through the control room,' Helmann said feebly.

Stein put his book down and swung his legs off his bunk. 'Have you checked Tube Six?'

'No, Mr Stein.'

'Wait here,' Stein said and walked toward the control room.

Anders ignored Stein as the second officer passed through.

A grim-faced Stein was back five minutes later. 'Is the captain asleep?'

Anders looked up from his clipboard. 'I don't think so. Why?'

Stein stepped through the watertight door and stopped outside Weiner's berth. 'I'm sorry to disturb you, kaleu,' he said loudly, 'but we have a man missing. Boatsman's Mate Bruch.'

Weiner's huge hand jerked back the green curtain. '*What?*' Alarm and disbelief spread across his usually good-humoured features. He leapt from his berth and dived into the control room where Anders was standing, white-faced, clutching his clipboard. Weiner's hand shook as he pulled the crew address microphone to his lips.

'Boatsman's Mate Bruch to report to the control room immediately. Boatsman's Mate Bruch to the control room at once.'

Weiner dropped the microphone and snapped his fingers for Anders' clipboard as Helmann appeared at the circular door. He seemed to have overcome his fear of officers for he said haltingly, 'He was good at splicing cables. He liked doing it, and he had been given the job of repairing the jumping wire. It had frayed by the first sheave, he said. A nice little job . . . Out in the open air . . . That's what he said . . .' Helmann's voice trailed off.

Silence in the control room. Weiner, his face haggard, took the clipboard from Anders' lifeless fingers and leafed through the documents, trying to read them with eyes that wanted to fill with tears as he thought of the girl running along the wharf, waving.

Anders managed to say, 'He was working on the forward casing.'

Weiner shook his head as if the nightmare would go away. 'Just before the crash dive?'

Anders nodded silently.

60

Brinkler turned from his dials and gauges. 'I'm sorry, kaleu. It was my fault. If I hadn't dived so quickly . . .'

'It wasn't your fault,' Stein said, brushing an invisible hair into place. 'Your job is to take the boat down quickly when the alarm sounds. The last man on the bridge should con the boat before closing the hatch.' Stein's cold eyes, staring hard at Anders, never wavered.

'I didn't ask for your opinion, Stein,' Weiner growled.

Stein turned. 'It's not an opinion, kaleu. I was quoting standing orders.'

Weiner's eyes glittered dangerously, but Anders spoke first.

'Do we turn back, kaleu? He might still be on the surface.'

'After six hours?' Stein asked sarcastically. 'I don't suppose he was wearing a life jacket?'

Weiner wheeled around to face Stein squarely. 'You're off watch, Mr Stein. Don't you need every minute of your free time to press your uniform?'

The insult drained the colour from Stein's face. He saluted Weiner stiffly and left the control room without speaking. Weiner looked at Anders. The younger officer had crumpled onto the chart stool and was staring at the floor, reminding Weiner of an abandoned marionette whose strings had been cut.

'Was he wearing his Drager?' Weiner asked, his voice soft.

Anders shook his head slowly.

'You know my regulations concerning men working on the deck casing,' Weiner snapped. 'Dragers *must* be worn at all times!'

There was another silence.

'Well,' Weiner said at length. 'It's for Flotilla HQ to decide whether or not we turn back.'

* * *

Weiner's request to be allowed to return and search the area where Bruch had been lost was refused by Lorient. If possible a minesweeper would be sent to the position, but *U700* was to continue to her patrol position south of Iceland.

That night *U700* lay stopped on the surface.

Anders, Stein, and the off-watch crew stood bare-headed while Weiner slowly recited a brief memorial service. The flowers scattered on the black, uncaring sea were made from tissue paper that had been dyed with coloured ink.

For Anders, that night marked the first of the many sleepless nights he would have to endure for the rest of his life.

20

By August 27, five days after she had left Lorient, *U700* neared her patrol position south of Iceland. The weather had been appalling for three days – days that with the steadily lengthening hours of daylight seemed to merge into a sustained hell of unremitting misery for every member of the crew.

Anders crawled into his bunk after four agonizing hours on watch, which he had spent lashed to the bridge with safety chains. There had been times during that watch when he thought it would be the easiest thing in the world to slip the quick-release catches and let the enraged seas take over his body and do what it liked with it.

His bunk was drenched with the condensation that ran down the bulkheads and was soaked up by his mattress like blotting paper. All his clothes were saturated with a foul-smelling mixture of urine, sweat, vomit, and condensation. He tried to sleep, but every time he closed his eyes his imagination painted a vivid picture of Boatsman's Mate Bruch clinging in panic and despair to the jumping wire as the boiling water rose higher and higher around his chest.

A violent roll heaved his limp body against the sodden bulkhead and sent his stomach surging into his throat. Just turn over and be sick, he thought. It wasn't worth the effort of trying to get up. But he turned the other way, taking care to keep his head on the same place on the pillow so that he wouldn't lose the carefully nurtured patch of wet warmth. At least he had his own bunk; not like the poor bastards forward and aft who had only one bunk between two men so that a man coming off watch had to crawl into the vomit-soaked blankets of the man going on watch. He tried to adjust the bunk's safety strap but his fingers wouldn't work as he wanted them to. He realized he was drifting off to sleep. He didn't want to sleep.

Sleep was where Bruch was waiting for him, crawling up the jumping wire from the swirling foam and reaching out with long, clutching fingers.

21

As exhaustion and seasickness dragged Anders into a fitful, nightmare-plagued sleep, 150 miles to the north at RAF Kaldadarnes in Iceland, Squadron Leader James Thompson of 269 Coastal Command squadron revved up the motors on his twin-engine Lockheed Hudson and taxied through the driving rain to the end of the desolate, levelled stretch of rock and lava that was jokingly referred to as an airstrip.

Slung against the Hudson's fuselage were a cluster of

the new air-borne depth charges that had replaced the 500 pound anti-submarine bomb – that unique weapon that was unable to sink submarines unless it was dropped down an open hatch. The only other armament the Hudson carried were nose and turret Browning 303 machine guns. The Hudson was a reasonably well-armed aircraft provided whatever it shot at didn't shoot back.

Five minutes later the twin-engined machine was air-borne and heading south under a sullen cloud base on what Thompson and his three-man crew imagined would be one more protracted and infinitely boring anti-submarine patrol in an equally boring war.

22

While Thompson was levelling off at 300 feet over the North Atlantic, Alan Brice in London was fast running out of patience. He had been six months in England; six months of shortages of just about every commodity imaginable, six months of having to spend virtually every night in the hotel bomb shelter while Goering's Luftwaffe droned overhead. His work at Newport was falling steadily behind. And he very much missed his wife and daughter. The chances of the British capturing a U-boat now seemed very remote, and he felt that he would be achieving more if he spent his time working on the problems of the magnetic torpedo back at the research station in Rhode Island.

He was about to leave his hotel room to send a cable to his boss, Admiral Swaffer, when there was a gentle tap at his door. It was another of Fleming's seemingly inexhaustible supply of attractive, but very proper, Wren drivers determined to show him the sandbagged sights of London.

This particular one had been given the task of taking him to Hampton Court.

'All the paintings have been moved somewhere safe,' she explained. 'But it's still well worth a visit. They're opening it specially for you.'

Brice sighed. The British were determined to keep him in England.

23

The nightmare of being awake was only slightly more tolerable than the nightmare of being asleep.

Anders opened his eyes and tried to focus them on the reading lamp. The only bodily motion he was aware of was the pressure of the safety strap as *U700* rolled. He heard the sound of breaking china from the galley and was surprised that there was anything left aboard the U-boat to break.

He closed his eyes for a moment and tried to divorce his body from the U-boat's gut-churning motion. Then he looked blearily at his watch. In fifteen minutes he would be relieving Stein in the control room. He released the strap and forced his aching limbs to move. The effort of sitting up exhausted him, and the movement of his body inside his clothes reminded him how wet and cold he was. The indescribable stench in the U-boat hit him like a blow in the solar plexus. He opened a locker and groped for some dry clothing, but everything his hand encountered was saturated. He pulled out a sweater with the vague idea of wrapping it around an exhaust pipe in the engine to dry out. The sleeve disintegrated in his hands. The garment was rotten – covered with the same fungus that the cook complained grew on a loaf of bread within a few hours of the can being opened.

He stood unsteadily in the companionway and nearly lost his balance when his foot skidded where someone had vomited. Clinging to the wardroom curtain, he offered a fervent prayer to be conveyed quickly to hell or to anywhere in the universe that wasn't the interior of a U-boat.

As expected, Stein was immaculate – even at the end of his watch. His sweater was spotless, and his hair neatly brushed. He smiled warmly at the dishevelled apparition that shuffled into the control room like a reluctant ghost.

'Good morning, Anders,' came the bright greeting. 'You're a few minutes early.'

U700 suddenly heeled. Anders grabbed a pipe, but Stein merely reached out a languid hand and gripped a safety strap. He watched Anders with a self-assured expression. 'Everything's in order. No news about Bruch.' It was the subject he always mentioned when Anders went on watch.

The next roll sent Anders staggering through the circular door to avoid the shame of being sick on the control room floor.

Thirty minutes after Anders had relieved Stein, Weiner appeared in the control room, red-eyed and unshaven. His appearance restored some of Anders' self-confidence, for he looked as if he had suffered worse than most.

'We're going to have to dive until the weather clears,' Weiner said thickly.

'We'll be late reaching our patrol position,' Anders tactfully reminded the older man.

'I've just paid a visit to the bow torpedo room. Thirty minutes into the watch, and they're all too ill to know what they're doing. I'd rather be late with a fit crew than on time with a boat manned by sick men.'

*   *   *

It was pleasant at 50 metres.

The U-boat seemed to be motionless as Brinkler eased it along at two knots, a speed that made depth-keeping easy for the hydroplane operators without putting an undue load on the batteries.

It was two hours since *U700* had dived out of reach of the weather. Her interior had been cleaned and disinfected, and there was a smell of coffee from the galley. Anders felt human again and, above all, warm. Weiner had loaned him a dry sweater that he kept in an airtight biscuit tin; a sensible idea that Anders resolved to copy on his next patrol.

Weiner was sitting on a stool at the chart table. 'Feeling better?' he asked.

'I'm beginning to think I might survive, kaleu.'

Weiner laughed and glanced at the chronometer. 'We'll come down again if it's no better – I promise.'

Chuckling to himself, Weiner heaved himself up the ladder into the small attack kiosk in the conning tower while Anders gave orders to take the boat up to periscope depth. Weiner perched on the swivel saddle and placed his eyes against the periscope visor. There was nothing to see but blackness, which would gradually change to pea-green and then light green as *U700* neared the surface. Then there would be a champagne swirl of sparkling bubbles, followed by the shock of seeing waves as the periscope head broke the surface. It was a phenomenon that Weiner knew he would never tire of seeing.

As soon as the periscope was clear of the surface, he would quickly scan through 360 degrees in case there were ships near enough to spot a periscope. If there were none, he would carefully search the horizon for distant ships that might be able to see a U-boat blowing its tanks and surfacing. While this was going on, the petty officer on the hydrophones would carefully listen for the beat of ships' propellers, and Anders would search for aircraft on the sky periscope. Only when all three men were satisfied that all was clear would Weiner call down the order: 'Standby to surface!' That was the theory.

Squadron Leader Thompson suppressed a yawn. Three hundred feet below was the unending monotony of the grey, windswept North Atlantic – a continuous blur of bleak, uninspiring nothingness. They hadn't even seen a sea-bird. Just water, water, and more water. His navigator, sitting frozen in the tail, drew a line across his chart and calculated the distance the Hudson had flown since his last fix. Thompson's gunner was sitting disconsolately in his turret nursing a cold Thermos flask and thinking about nothing in particular. The flight-sergeant was below, trying to find some music on his two radio sets. None of the men had said much since they had taken off from Iceland. Being in RAF Coastal Command, the Cinderella service, they had long since resigned themselves to fighting a forgotten war.

'Twenty metres,' Brinkler called.

There was a slight roll, the first indication apart from the depth gauges that *U700* was nearing the surface. Anders tightened his grip on the sky periscope when he sensed Stein was standing behind him.

'I thought you were off watch, Stein.'

'I heard you were surfacing. I could do with a breath of fresh air.'

It was a simple enough statement, yet Stein managed to make it sound like an insult. Anders was about to reply, but Stein was climbing the ladder to join Weiner in the conning tower.

'Fifteen metres,' Brinkler said. He was taking the U-boat up carefully. It was his job to make sure the bows didn't break the surface before the hydroplane operator trimmed off to run at periscope depth.

Anders noticed the first glimmer of green, diffused daylight through his periscope.

'Ten metres,' Brinkler said.

The radio operator pulled his headphones on and arranged his papers. He had several messages to transmit to Lorient as soon as the antenna was out of the water.

'No hydrophone effects,' the hydrophone operator droned.

Like Anders, Weiner could see green daylight and was bracing himself to rotate the attack periscope the instant it broke the surface.

'Five metres,' Brinkler intoned.

Both periscope heads burst into daylight at the same time. Weiner's first sweep revealed nothing. Anders quickly checked the grey, depressing bowl of sky and saw nothing but low, scudding cloud. He was about to start the slow, meticulous sweep when the radio operator suddenly let out a loud exclamation.

'It's Bruch!' he shouted excitedly. 'He's okay! That British seaplane picked him up! He's a prisoner-of-war but he's okay!'

Anders took his eyes away from the sky periscope and stared at the radio operator in disbelief.

'Bloody hell!' Thompson yelled. He hauled back on the control column, opened the throttles wide, and yanked the Hudson up into the cloud. The navigator bobbed up beside him.

'What's up, skipper?'

'Something down there,' Thompson said laconically. 'A long way off, but it was something that shouldn't be there.'

*   *   *

69

Anders returned his eyes to the periscope and completed his slow sweep of the sky. He cursed the U-boat's rolling, which made it difficult to obtain a steady image.

'Sky clear, kaleu,' he called up to Weiner.

Stein had to press himself against the side of the attack kiosk as Weiner swung around with the attack periscope.

The sea was empty. 'All clear, chief,' Weiner called down to Brinkler. 'Surface!'

There was a hiss of compressed air blasting into *U700*'s ballast tanks, flushing out the water and making the U-boat buoyant. Stein reached up to the hatch, ready to spin the handwheel as soon as the roar of water draining off the bridge stopped.

'Jesus bloody Christ,' Thompson's navigator breathed.

Thompson had dived out of the cloudbase. Two miles away the impossible was happening: a U-boat was blowing its tanks and surfacing as if it owned the entire bloody ocean.

And it was dead ahead.

Confident that Anders would sound the alarms if anything appeared, Weiner climbed through the hatch and on to the bridge followed by Stein.

'He's ours!' the flight-sergeant shouted ecstatically. 'He's ours, skipper. By Christ, we've got the bastard cold.'

Thompson's hand was already gripping the depth charge release control. 'Please, God,' he whispered, 'don't let him see me.'

The U-boat was 500 yards away. Two men had appeared on the bridge.

Weiner was about to lift the binoculars to his eyes when he heard the sound of the Hudson's Pratt and Whitney engines. Stein heard them at the same time. Both men spun around and gazed numb with horror at the aircraft that was charging straight at them at a height of less than 300 feet. It was so close that Weiner could see someone in the turret sitting behind the twin machine-guns.

'Down!' Weiner screamed giving Stein a kick that sent him staggering against the torpedo aimer.

Four objects detached themselves from the side of the Hudson's fuselage. For an insane moment Weiner thought that the pilot had released the bombs or whatever they were too early. But then he realized that they possessed the Hudson's momentum and were arching down, following a graceful but invisible curve that would end alongside *U700*.

The hours of low-level practice that Thompson had spent dropping smoke bombs paid off: it was a perfect straddle. A depth charge fell on each side of the U-boat, a third bounced off the bow, and the fourth plunged into the water by the stern. Thompson could hear his crew yelling jubilant congratulations as he banked the Hudson sharply to see what was going to happen. What happened exceeded his wildest dreams. With a tremendous WHUMMMP from the half ton of Torpex high explosive, four columns of water were hurled high into the air from beside the U-boat, lifting it bodily out of the water as if a huge hand from the depths had thrust it into the air. As the U-boat disappeared from view, hidden by the tons of water erupting into the sky, it seemed to the four dumbfounded men in the Hudson that the submarine was rolling on to its side as it fell back into the hollow where the sea had been blown away from beneath it.

A terrifying thunderclap smashed against Weiner's eardrums, driving the breath from his lungs and coherent thought from his mind. All that was left was a crude instinct

71

to survive; an instinct that enabled him to struggle up and cling grimly to the periscope standard.

He was dimly aware of the heeling bridge being surrounded by a curtain of water that was climbing into the sky. His legs were jelly, but he embraced the periscope standard with a strength that threatened to crack his ribs. There was a distant sound of men screaming. Water surged across the bridge and cascaded down the open hatch. He felt someone trying to drag his body away from the periscope, but it was the force of gravity; for the U-boat, which had lain over, was now righting itself. He saw Stein struggling to grab hold of something. Another second and he would be swept into the maddened sea. Weiner reached down and grabbed Stein's arm. With a superhuman effort he managed to haul the second officer against the periscope and hang on to him.

The Hudson roared over the U-boat for a second time. The spray was falling back. Thompson was astonished to see that although the U-boat had taken a direct hit by four depth charges, it was still miraculously afloat.

'They build 'em well,' the navigator commented as if reading his captain's thoughts.

'I'll show them just how well we build machine guns if they go for that twenty-millimetre,' was Thompson's grim reply as he pulled the Hudson around in a tight turn.

'What now, skipper? I thought those depth charges were supposed to be an improvement on the anti-sub bomb?'

'Shoot him up if he tries to dive,' Thompson answered.

'With 303s?'

But Thompson didn't reply. He pulled the Hudson out of the turn and aimed it straight at the U-boat.

If I can't sink the bastard, he thought, I can at least frighten it to death.

* * *

'No!' Weiner croaked when he saw men crawling out of the forward hatch. 'They'll kill you! Get back! Get back!'

The men hesitated and looked up in bewilderment at the diving aircraft. Weiner had been about to give the order to dive, but in that moment he realized there was only one thing he could do if he was to keep his men from getting killed.

'I don't believe it,' Thompson said. 'Someone wake me up.'

The U-boat was showing a white flag.

'Looks like a shirt,' the navigator said.

A signal lamp started flashing from the submarine's bridge.

'Typical navy types,' Thompson grumbled. 'How do they expect us to read that speed? In German too.'

'Hang on,' said the navigator. 'I think it's in English. Yes! It must be! W . . . E . . . Stop. H . . A . . V . . . E . . . Stop. S . . . U . . . R . . . It must be *survived! We have survived!*'

'Damn cheek,' Thompson said indignantly. 'Let's plaster them.'

'Wait! It's "surrendered", skipper!' the navigator yelled. 'We have *surrendered!*'

Thompson still didn't believe it. 'Signal them to send again,' he ordered.

The light flashed again from the U-boat.

'We have surrendered,' the navigator repeated.

Thompson groaned. It was unheard of for a U-boat to surrender to an aircraft.

'Now what do I do?' he complained.

Stein stared transfixed at the shirt and then at Weiner. He tried to speak down the voice pipe, but Weiner snapped the cover down.

'We've got to dive,' Stein said hoarsely.

'It's too late, Stein.'

Stein shook his head disbelievingly. He looked up at the Hudson that was warily circling its prey. A wild look came into his eyes. Before Weiner could move, he dived on to the wintergarten deck and swung the anti-aircraft guns toward the Hudson.

Weiner started after him. 'No, Stein! For God's sake! They'll kill you. They'll kill us all!'

'Let them!' Stein snarled, his expression blazing contempt and hatred.

Weiner tried to pull him away from the gun but was sent staggering backward by a savage kick in the stomach.

Almost immediately, the Hudson's engines opened up and it came diving down toward the U-boat with tongues of fire dancing on its nose. A stream of miniature waterspouts raced across the water. Weiner threw himself down and saw a row of holes stitch themselves across the deck casing. The roar of the aircraft's engines as it swept over the U-boat at 150 feet completely drowned Stein's cry of agony. He fell away from the gun clutching his left arm.

Weiner was on his feet. He grabbed the tails of the shirt that had wound themselves around the periscope and spread the signal out so that it could be seen more clearly.

24

It was a hot and humid afternoon in Berlin on that fateful August 27.

At 3:30 P.M. an enciphered Iceland/C-in-C Western Approaches, Liverpool intercept was placed on Kurt Weill's desk. He looked at the neat columns of code numbers and wondered why anything Iceland had to say would be of interest to Sir Percy Noble.

Weill was one of the senior cryptanalysts with Doenitz's Observation Service Beobachtung-Dienst, the little-known but vital decoding organization that had started to break the British Naval codes at the beginning of the war and had been breaking them ever since. The 'B-Service' now provided Doenitz with a daily intelligence summary on convoy sailing times, escort rendezvous positions, courses, speeds, and even cargoes.

Weill studied the signal flimsy for some minutes. It was the straightforward two-part code that had been in use by the British for a year, a dangerously long time, but with a code having to contain upward of 10,000 code numbers to be useful, it was understandable that the British were reluctant to change it.

Weill picked up his pencil and wrote down the substitutions for the numbers he recognized immediately:

4556 meant 'patrol'; 3087 meant 'aircraft'; 9927 meant 'Coastal Command'; and 6294 – the most frequently used code number of all, one that Weill saw every day – meant 'U-boat'.

Ten minutes later Weill had fifty per cent of the signal reduced to plain text: a U-boat had become involved with a Coastal Command Hudson. The aircraft had dropped depth charges on the U-boat, and the U-boat had 2773.

2773?

Weill frowned. 2773 hadn't been cracked. It wasn't in his cross-index or the monthly supplement. Nor did it appear in the day file.

Obviously it was a verb but what verb? Sink? Dive? Scuttle? Escape? But all those words were already covered by known code numbers. So what else was there that a U-boat could do? It had to be something surprising for

Coastal Command to trouble Sir Percy Noble with the news.

Weill thought for a minute. There was a remote chance that 2773 had been used by the British in a previous signal that had not been completely decoded. He crossed the office and slid back the cover on the first bank of the giant rotary card index. He punched 2773 on the selection keyboard and watched the huge drum slowly turn, flipping through the cards like a giant fairground machine. It stopped. The claw was holding the cards open at one that stated:

'2773. Used 5/5/40. HMS *Seal*/British Admiralty. See file UB/5/6/40.'

Weill recalled reading a story about HMS *Seal* but couldn't remember the exact details. He picked up his phone and asked for the library.

'Walter, maybe you can help me. What does HMS *Seal* mean to you?'

'Hold on.' Weill could hear a muffled conversation at the other end. Papers were shuffled. Then: 'Yes. She's a British submarine. Or rather, was.'

Weill's pulse quickened. 'What happened to her?'

'She surrendered last year in the Baltic to a trawler after her motors had been smashed by depth charges.'

Weill slowly replaced the phone and gazed at it for some moments. No wonder the code number wasn't frequently used. He placed the signal flimsy in front of him and slowly, almost reluctantly, filled in the substitution for 2773.

The next thing was to put a scrambled call through to Lorient. He wondered how Doenitz would react when he heard the news.

25

The radio operator was smashing the U-boat's cipher machine with a hammer as Anders climbed down into the control room.

'I want to send a message to headquarters.'

'Can't,' the radio operator said insolently, not looking up at the tall, spare officer. He brought the heavy hammer down on the machine's keyboard.

'Why not?'

'Because it's smashed – that's why not.'

The man was insubordinate, but Anders didn't have the will to argue. Ducking his head, he moved through the wardroom where a human chain were passing weighted bags along the boat for ejection through a torpedo tube. The men were silent but openly hostile by gesture and expression. He stopped outside Stein's berth and pulled back the curtain.

Stein looked up and tidied his hair with his free hand.

'I've come to see if the dressing is okay,' Anders said uncertainly.

'It's fine,' Stein muttered. Beads of perspiration stood out on his forehead. Blood was seeping through the makeshift sling on his left arm. His cold eyes watched Anders carefully.

'If you'd like another shot of morphine . . .'

'I'm okay!' Stein snapped.

There was a sudden hiss of compressed air being released into the boat as the contents of a torpedo tube were expelled. Stein made room for Anders on the bunk.

Anders sat and drew his bony knees up to his chin and stared at the floor.

'What's the Hudson doing?' Stein asked after a few seconds silence.

'Still circling.'

'Weiner?'

'Watching it.'

Anders broke the embarrassed silence that followed. 'How about the torpedo in Tube Three?'

'Jammed,' Stein replied in disgust. 'They tried everything to shift it. The bomb must've warped the tube.' He paused. 'You know which torpedo it is in that tube?'

Anders nodded. The two men were silent for a moment. 'Were they bombs or depth charges?' Anders said at length.

'One lousy five-hundred-pound anti-submarine bomb,' Stein said bitterly. 'Useless unless it scores a direct hit, and the only anti-submarine armament those Hudsons carry.'

'There were men on the deck casing,' Anders said. 'They were unprotected. If Weiner hadn't surrendered, they'd be dead now, and so would we if that Hudson had more depth charges.'

'The RAF hasn't got an air-borne depth charge, as you should know.'

Anders remembered how he had taken his eyes away from the sky periscope at the crucial moment during the surfacing procedure. 'It wasn't Weiner's fault,' he said suddenly.

The scar on Stein's face gleamed in the light from the reading lamp. The cold eyes fixed on Anders were unblinking. 'What wasn't?'

Anders opened his mouth to tell Stein about the moment when the news that Bruch was safe had come through. But his eyes met Stein's icy stare, and he knew that Stein wouldn't understand.

'What wasn't Weiner's fault?' Stein prompted.

Anders hesitated. 'Surfacing so near an aircraft. I wouldn't like to try to calculate the odds against it happening.' His voice ended on a miserable note.

'The odds that we could still shoot that Hudson down are pretty good,' Stein observed drily.

Anders stared at him. 'What do you mean? We've surrendered.'

'We have not surrendered,' Stein said harshly. 'Only Weiner has surrendered.' He handed Anders a sheet of paper.

We, the undersigned members of *U700* crew, deplore the surrender of our boat without a fight and urge Lieutenant Anders to arrest Captain Weiner and to countermand the surrender. We pledge Lieutenant Anders our total loyalty and will carry out whatever orders he issues to prevent this boat from falling into enemy hands.

Under the statement were some forty signatures arranged in a circle so that it was impossible to deduce who had signed first.

'Every member of the company has signed it,' Stein said.

'Everyone except me,' Anders said, eyeing the document with distaste.

'You don't have to sign it – just accept it.'

'Did they all sign willingly?'

'All that matters is that they signed.'

'Well I think it does matter,' Anders said evenly. 'Did you tell them when you twisted their arms that the captain did what he did to save their lives? That he didn't have

79

any choice but to surrender? Brinkler had told him we couldn't dive because the depth charges had jammed the 'planes. Did you tell them that?'

'All that matters now,' Stein said softly, 'is that this boat must be prevented from falling into enemy hands. We have the guns . . .'

Anders snorted. 'They'd rake the casings with machine-gun fire before we could get near them.' He pointed to Stein's sling. 'Look what happened to you.'

'We put the best gunners in the middle of the party,' Stein said smoothly.

'What party?' Anders asked suspiciously.

'The party that rushes the guns.'

It was some seconds before Anders realized what Stein was suggesting. He stared at him with a mixture of loathing and contempt. For once the twisted scar didn't worry him. 'You're insane!'

'I'm prepared to be a member of the shielding party, Anders.' He paused and smiled. 'Are you? Or are you as big a coward as Weiner?'

'Weiner surrendered because he wanted to save lives, including yours,' Anders said angrily. 'If I were to arrest him and order us to fight after having surrendered, I'd be denying all of us the protection of the Geneva Convention. The British would have the right to hang the lot of us like common criminals.'

Stein opened his locker, placed a Luger on the table, and pushed it toward Anders. The two men's eyes met. Choosing his words carefully, Stein said in a matter-of-fact tone, 'If you allow this boat to fall into enemy hands by *not* arresting Weiner, then I shall see to it that after the war you hang anyway – for cowardice.'

Anders returned to his berth and placed the Luger on his table. He stared at it as he listened to the signalmen smashing equipment. Three minutes passed before he made up his mind as to what he had to do.

Thompson studied the lone figure standing on the U-boat's bridge, staring back at the Hudson through binoculars.

'Wonder what the poor sod's thinking,' the navigator pondered.

'The same as me,' Thompson replied. 'He's probably wondering what will happen when we run low on fuel and have to leave him.'

'Shall I signal him to muster all his men on deck so we can keep an eye on them? They might be destroying stuff below.'

'They're bound to be,' Thompson agreed. 'But we're stopping him from scuttling by keeping them below.'

The flight-sergeant entered the cockpit.

'So?' Thompson demanded.

'A couple of armed trawlers and a destroyer, the *Burwell*, are on their way.'

'When?'

'Twenty-two hundred.'

Thompson groaned loudly. 'We'll be out of fuel long before then. What the devil do they think we're flying? A Zeppelin?'

The flight-sergeant grinned. 'We've been ordered not to run out of fuel until a Catalina turns up to relieve us. And if we have to leave before the Cat shows up, we have to destroy the U-boat.' The flight-sergeant became serious. 'Without warning, sir.'

Thompson's face went white. He turned in his seat. 'Why, for Christ's sake?'

'In case it tries to dive and escape,' the flight-sergeant said, avoiding Thompson's eyes.

26

Admiral Karl Doenitz's chiselled features were devoid of expression as he contemplated the plot table in the U-boat operation room at Lorient. Kneller stood behind him, nervously twisting and untwisting his fingers, glaring at the operations controller as if he were to blame for the astonishing news that had just been received from the B-Service codebreaking agency in Berlin.

'They definitely haven't got the U-boat's number?' Doenitz fired at the controller.

'No, admiral. They don't think it's in the British signal, but they've promised to call as soon as the decoding is complete.'

Doenitz continued gazing down at the giant map of the North Atlantic. There were markers for at least six U-boats that were within range of Hudsons operating out of Iceland. He turned to Kneller, his face perplexed. 'It just doesn't make sense, John – a U-boat surrendering to an aircraft. It's unheard of.'

'We could call up all boats and ask for situation reports,' Kneller suggested.

Doenitz permitted himself a rare smile. 'The British are extremely clumsy. No U-boat *has* surrendered. If one has been damaged so that it couldn't dive, then the captain would obey the battle orders by scuttling.'

The controller looked baffled. 'Then why have the RAF in Iceland sent that signal to England?'

'Because the British are testing their code security,' Doenitz replied. 'All their monitoring stations are now tuned to forty-nine, ninety-five kilocycles – our main

U-boat frequency – to see if we suddenly start sending a flurry of signals to all boats.'

There was a relaxing of tension in the room; Doenitz's explanation made good sense.

'What the British signal won't include,' Doenitz continued, 'is the position of the U-boat. For the simple reason that the British don't know the position of any of our U-boats.'

The controller's phone rang. He picked it up. His face clouded with worry as he listened.

'Yes . . .' He scribbled rapidly on a pad.

There was a total silence in the room.

'Thank you for decoding it so quickly,' the controller said. 'Yes, he's with me now. I'll tell him.' He carefully replaced the phone and tore the sheet of paper off the pad.

Kneller took it from him and handed it to Doenitz who glanced at it and then impassively picked up one of the long cues. He rested the tip near London on the Greenwich Meridian.

'Thirty degrees west,' Doenitz said, reciting tonelessly.

The tip moved westward across England and stopped in mid-Atlantic.

'Sixty-one degrees north.'

The tip moved north toward Iceland. It came to rest pointing at the marker for a U-boat.

U700.

The long, stunned silence that followed was broken by Kneller.

'We've nothing that can reach it before dark,' he muttered. 'Even before dark at that latitude.'

27

There was an uncomfortable bulge in Anders' pocket as he climbed through the hatch onto *U700*'s bridge. Weiner was alone, hunched over the coaming, watching the Hudson. He looked around to see who the newcomer was and then returned to watching the aircraft. His good-humoured features were lined with anxiety. Anders was uncertain what to say and embarrassed by what he knew he had to do: place Weiner under arrest.

'It was a day like today,' Weiner said without turning around. 'Except there was thirty metres of water under *U700*'s keel instead of three thousand.' His voice was flat and unemotional, as if he were trying to relate the events without having to think about them. 'I'd joined *U700* the week before. A new command. Engineers were still working on her when I took her out for her first torpedo-firing trial. We trimmed off at periscope depth, and I gave the order to fire Tube Three. There was the usual popping in your ears caused by compressed air being released into the boat.'

Anders slowly eased the Luger from his pocket and released the safety catch.

Weiner paused for a moment, collecting his thoughts. 'Suddenly there were shouts and commotion from the forward torpedo room. Brinkler had compensated for loss of trim when the torpedo was fired, but he found that he couldn't hold her. She was going down by the bow. I rushed forward. Six men were trying to hold the broken torpedo door in place. Water was flooding into the boat. Then the pressure blew the door right off. The water was a raging torrent. In a few seconds the entire boat would be flooded.'

Weiner passed a hand over his face. Anders took a step toward Weiner and aimed the Luger at his captain's back. The steadiness of his hand surprised him.

'There was only one thing to do – close the watertight door as fast as possible. A torpedo hadn't been secured – it had rolled off the rack so that the men couldn't get to the door anyway. Something was stopping the door from closing. It looked like a piece of rag or something. I seized an axe and hacked at it. I hacked and hacked. Suddenly it came away, and the door closed.' Weiner stopped.

'What was it?' Anders asked, guessing the answer.

'A hand,' Weiner said flatly.

Anders could see sweat trickling down the older man's temple.

'We left through the aft hatch which was above water. Divers pumped the forward compartment out and *U700* continued with her trials a week later. Faulty welding around the torpedo door's hinge they said.'

'But you saved the boat and everyone else aboard,' Anders said quietly.

Weiner's laugh was hollow. 'That's what they said. They even gave me a medal. I threw it away. They wouldn't give a medal to those poor bastards trapped in the torpedo room because they said they hadn't done anything.' Weiner paused, adding sarcastically, 'Hadn't done anything. They only died, that's all.'

'What do you want to do now, kaleu?'

Weiner continued to stare at the Hudson. 'I'm not letting the British set foot on this boat. I'll go down and fire the scuttling charges as soon as everyone is safely off.'

'The British might not let you.'

'They will,' Weiner replied. 'They respect the tradition

of the captain being the last to leave. Except that I won't leave.'

Weiner turned and saw the Luger that Anders was holding levelled at his chest.

The navigator in the Hudson was puzzled. 'What are those two playing at down there?'

'What does it matter?' Thompson asked irritably. He pulled the Hudson out of the continuous circle it had been maintaining ahead of the U-boat and lined his machine up for the final approach. 'All I know is, no matter who wins this bloody awful war, no history book is going to have a kind word to say about us or the order we've been instructed to carry out this day.'

Thompson's hand went to the depth charge release control.

Weiner seemed saddened rather than surprised by the sight of the Luger.

'I'm sorry, kaleu,' Anders said.

'Why?'

'I have to place you under arrest.'

'Why be sorry if you're convinced you're doing the right thing? Or has Stein convinced you?'

'I have no choice.'

Weiner spread his stubbly fingers along the wind deflector and gazed up at the white shirt hanging from the periscope standard. 'That's the story of Germany, Anders – no choice. What do you plan doing?'

'Cancel the surrender and fight.' Then Anders was pleading with Weiner. 'Kaleu, if only you would do it. We could say that the surrender was a ruse of war. We could open fire on the Hudson. We could . . .' Anders' voice trailed into silence as Weiner shook his head.

Neither of the two men had noticed that the watchful

Hudson had stopped circling and was now approaching the U-boat.

'You're too late, Anders,' Weiner said, looking beyond the younger man's shoulder and smiling faintly. 'Too late.' Weiner pointed to the horizon.

'Hold it, skipper,' the Hudson's navigator called. 'What's he pointing at down there?'

Thompson's eyes went to the U-boat's bridge. One of the two Germans was pointing at something. Thompson craned his neck.

There was a smudge of smoke on the horizon. An armed trawler, the first of a small fleet of British warships converging on *U700*, had arrived.

28

At nine o'clock the following morning, August 28, Ian Fleming left his office at the Admiralty in London and took a taxi to Alan Brice's hotel. He found the American scientist eyeing a plate of kidneys.

'You won't believe this,' Fleming began.

'I've just tried the coffee,' Brice said. 'So I'm now in the sort of receptive mental state to believe anything.'

'We've captured a U boat.'

'*Almost* anything,' Brice amended. 'Would you like my breakfast?'

'No thanks. I'm trying to live without American aid. It surrendered yesterday. South-west of Iceland.'

Brice put down his fork and stared at Fleming in surprise. 'You've finally done it.'

'It surrendered to Coastal Command,' Fleming said sadly.

'Is that so bad?'

'How would you feel if one of your lab cleaners won a Nobel prize for physics?'

Brice considered. 'I get your point. So what did they do to accomplish this amazing feat?'

'Nothing really. They just chucked a few depth charges at it. Coastal Command's policy of attacking anything afloat, friend or foe, has finally paid off. It'll be a long time before the navy forgives them.'

'Is it damaged?' Brice inquired.

'Our reputation?'

'The U-boat.'

'Slight damage to her hydroplanes so that she couldn't dive, but nothing that her crew couldn't've put right in a few minutes.'

Brice frowned. 'So why did she surrender?'

Fleming shrugged. 'Search me, old boy. Maybe the captain felt sorry for Coastal Command. No one on our side likes them.'

'Any torpedoes aboard?' Brice asked hopefully.

'That's the bad news. The boarding party have reported a spare warhead in the forward torpedo room. That's all.'

'Probably with an old contact firing pistol,' Brice said regretfully. 'They would've dumped it if it was a magnetic head.' The scientist looked up at Fleming. 'Even so, I'd sure like a chance to take a look at the sub. Will that be possible?'

Fleming looked uncertain.

'Look, Ian – I've seen enough castles and palaces. You haven't got a Wotan warhead but you have got a German U-boat which I'll happily settle for. After that I'd like to go home.'

'I thought you were enjoying yourself? All our girls are

throwing themselves at Americans. The night life . . .'

Brice gave a sour smile. 'How in hell can one enjoy the night life in a city that never gets dark?'

Fleming laughed at the reference to the double summer-time emergency wartime measure. In June there had been bright sunshine at 10:30 P.M.

'So about the sub?' Brice prodded.

'I'll see what I can do, old boy,' Fleming promised.

'What's happening to it now, or is that a secret?'

'It's a secret,' Fleming admitted. 'But I can tell you she's being towed to Iceland.'

29

'Iceland,' Doenitz said in disgust. He handed the decoded signal that had just been received from Paris back to Kneller and surveyed the plot table moodily.

'Well,' Kneller said with finality. 'There's nothing we can do about it there.'

Doenitz's expression became thoughtful. 'John, when we captured the HMS *Seal* last year what was the first thing we did with it?'

'We handed it over to the experts for them to look at.'

'And who were they?'

Kneller thought for a moment 'I'm not sure, probably Blohm and Voss.'

'Exactly,' Doenitz said. 'Blohm and Voss, our largest submarine construction yard.' He seized a cue and jabbed the tip at Iceland. 'And the British equivalent of Blohm and Voss is . . .' Doenitz swept the cue eastward to the north-west coast of England, '. . . the Vickers submarine works at Barrow-in-Furness. Right on the edge of the Lake District.' He looked at Kneller in triumph, the light of battle shining in his eyes. 'And Barrow, John, *must* be within reach of a dive bomber fitted with long-range tanks!'

Kneller looked doubtful. He hated to disillusion the admiral, but it had to be said. 'With respect, admiral, the navy doesn't have a dive bomber, and Marshal Goering is the only man apart from the Fuehrer with the authority to loan us one. Personally, I don't think he will.'

Doenitz thought hard. 'We can't allow that U-boat to remain intact in enemy hands.'

'I appreciate that, admiral, but . . .'

'I shall fly to Karinhall and visit him,' Doenitz interrupted. 'God knows, I can't stand the man, but I have no choice.'

30

'Things are beginning to look interesting,' commented Ian Fleming as he and Brice strolled to the first hole on Coombe Hill golf course. 'A book found on *U700* has upset Franklin D. He was shown a copy yesterday.'

Brice was intrigued. 'What sort of book?'

'The crew destroyed just about every document on the U-boat except one. Perhaps they didn't think it important – probably because they never looked at it. It was a ship recognition guide – silhouettes – that sort of thing.'

Brice stopped walking. 'And that was considered important enough to show to the president?'

Fleming grinned. 'All the silhouettes were of the US Navy's capital ships with detailed information on the location of magazines and the best points along hulls to aim torpedoes at.'

Brice whistled.

'It's got Roosevelt hopping mad,' Fleming continued. 'Just the excuse he was looking for to step up the US Navy's belligerent neutral attitude to U-boats. From now on there's to be even closer co-operation between your navy and ours in the war against U-boats.'

The news astonished Brice. 'You're kidding. American warships are going to hunt and sink U-boats?'

'Good Lord no, old boy. But if one of your ships or aircraft spots one, they'll now fall all over themselves to tell us where it is.' Fleming paused and smiled. 'As soon as *U700* is brought to this country, you're to have unlimited access to it. Mr Churchill's orders.'

Brice was pleased. 'That's great. Hey, maybe I could talk to her crew? What about her torpedo officer?'

Fleming looked doubtful. 'Highly irregular, and besides, they're hardly talking to us. The interrogators are still beavering away at the captain, the second officer's in hospital with a shot up arm, and the first officer's on his way to a prisoner of war camp somewhere in England.'

Part Two

31

It was early September and already summer was losing its grip on the landscape as the first colours of autumn seeped into the trees that huddled in the valleys and stood alone on the high fells.

Anders had been awake for fifteen minutes, watching the passing scenery from the train window and wondering how far north they had come during the long night that had consisted of periods of fitful sleep disturbed by jerking shunts as locomotives were changed at an assortment of darkened stations.

Major Shulke, the dapper army officer who had been marched at gunpoint into his carriage after trying to escape the previous evening at Euston Station, was still sound asleep – watched by two resentful guards who sat at the far side of the reserved compartment with their hands resting on their rifles.

Anders caught a brief glimpse through the hills of sunlight burning on an expanse of water. A lake.

Shulke stirred and stretched. The two guards became more alert and tightened their grips on their rifles.

Shulke opened his eyes. 'Good morning, Bernard,' he said cheerfully.

'Good morning, Conrad. You slept well. I envy you.'

'Where are we?'

'I don't know. There's a huge lake over there.'

Shulke yawned and allowed the warm morning sun to

bathe his face. His hand dropped casually on to the window strap. The guards sat forward, watching him intently.

'You've upset them again,' Anders said.

Shulke smiled mischievously. 'I escaped again during the night while all three of you were snoring.'

Anders looked at the little major in astonishment.

'Hopped out through this window at a station,' Shulke said sleepily. 'The one with the long legs caught me at the end of the platform.' He winked at the taller of the two guards. Neither of them were amused. 'I wonder if they understand German?'

'Lucky you weren't shot,' Anders said chuckling.

'I zig-zagged.'

'Did you get the name of the station?'

'Of course,' Shulke said haughtily. 'Bovril.'

Anders and Shulke clutched the sides of the swaying army truck as it bumped along a narrow, rutted track through a dense forest of tall, depressing pines where the summer sunshine didn't reach. They had stopped talking as soon as the truck had turned off the main road. Both men were thinking the same thing: a truck with two prisoners driving deeper and deeper into a forest where shots would not be heard.

Shulke took a chance on the guards being unable to understand German. 'We make a break for it as soon as the truck stops. I'm not going to let these swine shoot me like a horse with a broken leg. I'd rather be shot while running.'

'They won't,' Anders said, pointing at the oppressive forest. 'Barbed wire if you look carefully. See?'

Shulke looked. Anders was right; where the bracken was dying down it was possible to discern the ugly gleam of skilfully positioned barbed wire entanglements threading through the trees.

'Why would they bother with barbed wire if they're going to shoot us?' Anders asked.

A shout and a gesture from one of the guards made it plain that the two prisoners were not to talk.

Shulke shivered. He noticed a tower rising above the gloomy pines.

'For fire watching,' Anders said quietly. 'But you can bet they've got searchlights and machine-guns up there.'

The truck stopped at a heavy, mesh-covered steel gate that stretched across the road. Two soldiers carefully checked the driver's documents before opening the gate and waving the vehicle through.

The trees thinned out and finally gave way to a pleasant, neatly trimmed hedge that lined each side of the track. The two prisoners experienced a sense of relief now that the truck was in the sun again.

'Looks like some sort of approach road,' Shulke said, half-standing to peer around the side of the truck.

Then came the shock: the army vehicle rounded a bend and drove down the side of a magnificent country mansion with an imposing gabled roof crouching protectively over ivy-covered walls. The truck boomed through an enclosed, cobbled stableyard where the walls of the mansion suddenly broke out in a rash of pipes and gutters that climbed the brickwork like varicose veins. Anders caught a glimpse of heavy bars and steel mesh covering upper windows. Then the truck was through an arch and into the sunlight again – and into another world.

The two prisoners could only stare in amazement, for it was a world of clipped lawns, gravelled paths, pleasant wooded slopes, and immaculate vegetable plots where an overall-clad army of gardeners were at work with hoes and rakes. At the foot of the wooded slopes was the spectacular sweep of a broad, hill-fringed lake.

The truck stopped. The guards jumped out and

motioned for the two prisoners to do likewise. Anders and Shulke climbed down from the tailboard and stood uncertainly, clutching the army-issue kitbags that contained their few possessions. The guards gave their charges a final scowl and jumped back on to the truck. First gear was crunched home, and the truck rumbled off through the stableyard.

'Now what happens?' Anders asked.

'Look!' Shulke said, pointing at a group of men who appeared to be inspecting the gardeners' handiwork.

'What?'

'Their uniforms!'

It was then that Anders realized why he hadn't seen anything that was so unusual about the men: they were wearing Luftwaffe, Wehrmacht, and Kriegsmarine uniforms. Common enough in Germany, not so common in England.

'You don't suppose that the British have made a mistake do you?' Shulke wondered as a whistling *korvettenkapitän* walked past pushing a wheelbarrow loaded with vegetables.

'Good morning,' a cheerful voice said.

The new arrivals turned. Coming down the broad flight of steps that led to the mansion's main entrance was a fresh-faced Luftwaffe lieutenant holding an official-looking clipboard.

Shulke and Anders regarded him solemnly.

'I shouldn't stand in the middle of the road,' the lieutenant warned. He consulted his clipboard. 'You must be Major Conrad Shulke and Lieutenant Bernard Anders?'

The two prisoners agreed that they were.

'Excellent,' the airman said. 'I'm Paul Faulk.'

He got no further for at that moment an ancient station wagon of indeterminate ancestry roared around the corner of the building from the direction of the stableyard. Its tyres scrabbled wildly on the loose gravel as the driver hauled the vehicle's heavy rear end straight with a neat handbrake turn. The engine opened up and the station wagon charged forward. Shulke and Anders grabbed their kitbags and jumped for safety in opposite directions as the vehicle braked to a standstill. Anders was surprised to see that the driver was a young woman aged between twenty and twenty-five, wearing what appeared to be a nurse's uniform.

'Lieutenant Faulk,' she said accusingly, ignoring the two prisoners she had nearly mown down. 'It's still not right. The brakes make a dreadful noise, and the engine still over-revs when I press the clutch.' Her German was slow but correct.

Faulk looked concerned. 'Well, we didn't promise to be able to cure it, nurse. But I'll get them to have another look.'

'Oh don't bother,' the woman said. 'Sorry I frightened you just then. New arrivals?'

'Yes, miss,' Shulke said.

The young woman smiled. She was brunette, poised and self-confident. 'Don't forget that we drive on the left in this country.'

Anders smiled. 'I don't suppose we'll get the chance to do much driving.'

'I was thinking of your curb drill,' the woman said briskly. She let out the clutch and drove toward a group of low buildings that were a hundred yards from the main building.

Faulk crossed to Anders and Shulke. 'Nurse Lillian Baxter,' he explained. 'She visits the hall several times a week from Barrow. She once told me that she opted for German rather than French at school, so watch what you say in front of her.'

'Her driving will ensure that she's never short of clients,' Shulke observed drily.

Faulk chuckled. 'She doesn't have to take a driving test – the British have scrapped them in order to make their country too dangerous to invade.'

The three men laughed. It was the first time in days that Anders felt the tension beginning to unwind.

'One small point,' Shulke said. 'Presumably this is a prisoner of war camp?'

Faulk was surprised. 'Yes, of course.' He pointed to the low buildings. 'You'd better report to Major Veitch's office while I see about your quarters.'

Sergeant Rogers of the Black Watch looked up from his desk. 'Shulke and Anders?'

'Yes,' Shulke replied.

Rogers tapped on a door marked 'Major J. R. Veitch' and entered. He emerged a few seconds later and held the door open. 'Your senior officer is with Major Veitch, but he'd like to see you now.'

Major James Reynolds Veitch of the Grenadier Guards was a tall, spare man in his mid-forties. He half rose from his chair as the two men were ushered into his office. Anders heard the door close softly behind him.

There was a high-backed chair facing Veitch's desk. All Anders could see of the chair's occupant were long, sensitive fingers holding a smoking cheroot and the cuff of a well-cut Kriegsmarine jacket.

Veitch briskly introduced himself and held his hand out to the man in the chair. 'And this is your senior officer . . .'

Anders didn't hear the rest of Veitch's sentence, for the man had stood and Anders found himself staring at a hawk-like nose and into a pair of compelling, unblinking eyes.

The senior German officer at Grizedale Hall was Otto Kretschmer.

32

'You've probably noticed,' Major Veitch said, 'that this is no ordinary prisoner of war camp. It's the first, the first of many most likely, that we've established for German officers. For non-National Socialist officers that is.' He selected his words carefully, keeping his eyes on Anders and Shulke to gauge the effect his words were having.

'And just in case you two have sympathies in that direction that weren't discovered when you were screened, let me say here and now that Nazi bullying is one thing that the commander and I will not tolerate under any circumstances. If there are incidents, those responsible will be sent to one of the camps that the Free Polish run, and we don't ask them too many questions on the way they choose to run their operation. So, if you want to stay here and be treated as officers, then it's up to you to behave like officers. You will find that you have reasonable freedom of movement inside the wire. Tunnelling is out of the question because Grizedale Hall is built on rock.'

Veitch paused and smiled faintly. 'My men look after perimeter security, and the commander is responsible for internal discipline among the prisoners. I've also heard that he's the chairman of the escape committee.'

Not a muscle in Kretschmer's face moved.

'Standard punishment for escape attempts is the maximum permitted under the Geneva Convention,' Veitch continued. 'Twenty-eight days in the punishment block. There's an army nurse on my staff who has her sick-bay on the ground floor of the hall. Finally, there's the hall itself – one of the finest in the country. After the war the army will have to restore it to its rightful owners in good condition, so if it's damaged in any way, the War Office will be only too pleased to rehouse you in huts. Any questions?'

Anders and Shulke had none. Anders had kept his eyes on the floor during Veitch's speech to avoid having to look at Kretschmer.

'Very good,' Kretschmer said, speaking for the first time. 'See Lieutenant Faulk about your quarters.' The unwavering eyes turned to Anders. 'Ask him to show you where my office is please, Anders. I'd like to see you in one hour precisely.'

33

While Anders was waiting for his interview with Otto Kretschmer, a Junkers 52 tri-motor transport aircraft took off from a small airfield near Lorient in western France and set a course for Germany.

The aircraft was the personal transport of Admiral Karl Doenitz. Accompanying him was his aide, John Kneller. The two men had arranged a meeting with the one person who could, if he wished, provide the navy with an aircraft that was capable of reaching and destroying *U700*.

34

'How is the admiral?' was Kretschmer's first question.

Anders glanced at the horseshoe fixed to the wall behind Kretschmer's gaunt head. It had been covered with gold chocolate paper and was the only decoration in the small, bare room that served as an office.

'He seemed well when I last saw him.' Anders could feel the dark eyes watching him dispassionately.

'What happened to your boat?'

The inevitable question, Anders thought. 'We were bombed by an aircraft.'

'Casualties?'

'One man was wounded in the arm.' Anders wondered if Kretschmer knew the truth about *U700*.

'Can you remember the last tonnage sunk figures?' Anders relaxed. Kretschmer apparently knew nothing. 'May and June was around six hundred thousand tons. July was very low – about a hundred thousand tons.'

'What about your boat?'

A pause.

'Well?' Kretschmer pressed.

'Nothing,' Anders said awkwardly.

Kretschmer's eyebrows went up. 'Nothing?'

'It was our first patrol.'

Kretschmer drummed his fingers on the desk, aware that the slender young officer was steadfastly refusing to meet his eyes. He opened a drawer and spread a British newspaper on his desk. Anders could see a pencil ring around a news item.

'We sometimes obtain newspapers from the guards in

103

exchange for Red Cross chocolate,' Kretschmer explained. 'Did the British hold you in the same interrogation centre as Captain-Lieutenant Weiner?'

The question surprised Anders. 'No.'

Kretschmer regarded him for some seconds and then tapped the newspaper. 'Can you read English?'

'With difficulty.'

'So you don't know about Weiner?'

Anders shook his head, suspecting that Kretschmer was playing with him.

'Weiner hanged himself,' Kretschmer said abruptly. 'Why do you think he did that? *U700* fought didn't it?'

Anders gaped at him in disbelief. It was a moment before he could collect his reeling thoughts. 'I – I don't know why. We fought . . . We used our anti-aircraft guns.'

'I'm sorry to be the one to tell you,' Kretschmer said sympathetically. 'The story merely says that U-boat commander Hans Weiner was found hanged in his cell.'

Anders stared miserably down at the floor, and Kretschmer realized little was to be gained by pressing the young man for more information. 'You've seen the nurse for medical inspection?'

Anders nodded.

'Very well,' Kretschmer said. 'First thing after breakfast tomorrow, you will report to Lieutenant Paul Faulk to be allocated a gardening schedule.'

Anders rose like a man in a trance.

'One thing more,' Kretschmer said. 'Was Richard Stein held at the same centre as you?'

'No, commander.'

'Well, I don't suppose the British will send him here.' Kretschmer dropped the newspaper in his drawer and slammed it shut. The interview was over.

Outside in the corridor, Anders leaned against the wall

and closed his eyes; his betrayal of Weiner was now irrevocable. His death had extinguished the spark of hope that one day, somehow, Anders would be able to confess, and that Weiner would understand.

35

The music stopped abruptly, and the girl froze in mid-dance step. Her chiffon veils continued to swirl about her body in the heat thrown out from the crackling log fire in the massive hearth that occupied one wall of the vast banqueting hall. She watched the SS captain pick up the bull-whip and advance slowly to the middle of the floor, which the Luftwaffe and SS officers had cleared for the entertainment. They were totally silent, sitting in a semicircle, watching the girl intently.

The SS captain twisted his lips in a parody of a smile and slowly coiled the bull-whip's long, vicious leather thong around his fingers. The girl pushed her long, blonde hair away from her face and raised her eyes from the whip to those of the captain's as if seeking mercy. But there was none.

The SS captain flicked his wrist, and the tip of the whiplash landed lightly on the girl's bare foot. She flinched but kept her balance. The captain made a few deliberate movements to position the thong across the floor to his satisfaction. The girl watched it as though it were a snake – her face white, her eyes wide with terror. The only sound in the hall was the splutter and crackle of the huge log fire whose twisting flames silhouetted the girl's graceful body through her transparent veils.

The SS captain tensed. There was a sudden blur of

movement followed by a loud crack. A strip of the girl's chiffon fluttered to the floor exposing pale shoulders to the circle of greedy eyes. There was an outburst of wild applause. The music started, and the now smiling girl resumed her erotic dance.

Reichsmarshal Hermann Goering stopped clapping and poured a drink for his guest. 'What do you think of my magnificent Karinhall, admiral? Just the place for week-end houseparties, eh?'

Doenitz was sitting uncomfortably on the edge of his chair and making a poor attempt at concealing his disapproval at what was going on. He looked at the obese figure, resplendent in a white dress uniform, and smiled politely. 'A magnificent building, marshal,' he agreed.

The music stopped. The whip cracked, and another strip of chiffon fluttered to the floor. There was loud cheering as the music started again.

Goering watched the pirouetting girl with an amused smile. 'They're a husband and wife team you know. I saw their act in a Berlin night club. Clever don't you think?'

Doenitz remained silent.

Goering drained his glass and twirled the stem in his pudgy fingers. 'You still haven't told me why we have the pleasure of this visit, admiral.'

Doenitz hesitated and then decided to come straight to the point. 'I need the loan of a bomber together with an aircrew and ground crew for three days, marshal.'

The bull-whip cracked loudly, stripping more chiffon from the girl.

'What sort of bomber?' Goering inquired mildly as the girl began dancing again.

'A dive bomber. One capable of carrying a thousand-kilo bomb for two thousand kilometres, delivering it, and returning.'

Goering shook his head sadly. 'My dear admiral, I need

a thousand such bombers for my Luftwaffe – two thousand – three thousand!'

The bull-whip cracked twice – and the girl was suddenly naked. She covered her breasts with her arm, but the captain skilfully flicked the tip of the whip around her wrist and drew her hand to one side. He reversed the handle so that it was pointing at the girl and started pulling her toward him.

Goering turned his small, cunning eyes on Doenitz. 'Why a dive bomber, admiral?'

'For accuracy.'

'Ah. A small target?'

The girl stood motionless, legs slightly apart as the SS captain moved the bull-whip's handle toward her. She gave a little shudder as it lightly brushed against the side of her neck. And then it moved downward, between her breasts, across her stomach, and down the outside of her left thigh. Doenitz opened his mouth to speak, but Goering silenced him with a finger held to his moist lips. The bull-whip's handle began moving up the inside of the girl's thigh.

'A small target,' Doenitz agreed, irritated at having been silenced.

Goering smiled mischievously. 'About sixty metres by six metres, say?'

Doenitz looked up sharply. Goering seemed to be gently mocking him. 'About that size,' he said stiffly, wondering just how much the fat air marshal knew.

The bull-whip's handle completed its journey, and the girl began a writhing motion with a circular movement from her hips.

'Admiral,' Goering said spreading his hands like a magician trying to convince his audience of his honesty. 'If I had such an aircraft, I'd be only too delighted to lend it to you for as long as you needed it. But I haven't.'

The girl's hips were moving faster and she was making

low moaning noises from the back of her throat. She dropped backward onto her hands, but the SS captain kept the bull-whip's handle in position.

Goering smiled beguilingly. 'But if you have a special target in mind, then my Luftwaffe might be willing to consider a mass raid which would be certain to destroy this . . .' Goering smiled again, '. . . sixty metre target of yours.'

The girl let out a loud, gasping cry and slipped to the floor as her arms and legs lost the strength to support her weight. A light rash appeared on her chest under the glistening film of perspiration as the audience rose to their feet clapping and cheering.

'A remarkable climax to a brilliant act,' Goering said smugly, raising his voice above the uproar.

Doenitz put down the drink he hadn't touched and stood.

'You must excuse me, marshal, but I have to make an early start in the morning.'

Goering hauled himself to his feet. 'But my dear admiral, surely you'll stay for the morning hunt?'

'I'm extremely sorry, marshal,' Doenitz said politely. 'I am most grateful for your hospitality but I must return to France.'

The Ju52 took off from Goering's private airstrip at 9:00 the following morning and headed back to Lorient.

'One dive bomber,' Doenitz said bitterly as he stared down at the forest rolling past under the port wing. 'One dive bomber. My God, you'd think I'd asked him for a squadron on permanent loan.'

Kneller looked sympathetic. 'Did he come out with his favourite expression?'

'Everything that flies belongs to me,' Doenitz mimicked and lapsed into a brooding silence.

'He still hasn't forgiven you over those Kondors,' Kneller said.

'He suspects something,' Doenitz said.

Kneller was surprised. 'How?'

'I don't know. I'm certain he doesn't know all the details, but he will. It makes the destruction of *U700* even more urgent – before he goes crawling to Hitler with his own account of its surrender. One aircraft! One!'

Doenitz lapsed into a brooding silence staring pensively out of the window at the tri-motor's port engine. Then he turned and allowed his gaze to travel slowly around the aircraft's spacious interior. He stiffened and moved forward on to the edge of his seat. 'John,' he said thoughtfully. 'Tell Goder that I'd like a word with him.'

Lieutenant Hans Goder – one of the navy's few pilots – handed over control to his co-pilot Max Hartz and followed Kneller into the main cabin. The two men looked down in surprise at Admiral Doenitz who was on his knees examining the aircraft's floor.

'Ah, Goder,' Doenitz said, standing and kicking the carpet back into place, 'sit down.'

The admiral made himself comfortable.

'You and Hartz have been flying me around Europe for the best part of a year now. What's been our longest trip?'

'Berlin to Rome, admiral,' Goder said, wondering what this was leading up to.

It was Kneller who began to have an inkling of what was on his admiral's mind. He looked alarmed and was about to open his mouth, but Doenitz silenced him with a gesture.

'Mm, a Ju52,' Doenitz said. It was the work horse of Germany. One of the sturdiest, most reliable aircraft ever built. 'What's its maximum range?'

Goder considered. 'About two thousand kilometres with a low payload say, fifteen hundred kilos, admiral.'

Doenitz leaned forward in a confiding manner. 'I want

it to carry a payload of that weight but twice the distance. Would that be possible?'

'*Four thousand* kilometres?' Goder gaped at Doenitz in astonishment.

'Is it possible? Could it be lightened?'

It was Goder's turn to look around the cabin. 'Well,' he said doubtfully. 'I suppose it would be possible to reduce its weight drastically, admiral. Bulkheads could be taken out – extra tanks fitted. Yes, it might be possible.'

Doenitz looked delighted and even managed a smile, the first Kneller had seen since the *U700*'s surrender.

'What sort of payload have you in mind, admiral?' Goder asked tentatively.

'A torpedo,' Doenitz replied with satisfaction.

36

It was an hour since the night raid had started, and still the droning bombers were pounding London. After so many months in London, Alan Brice had learned to do what everyone else in the very opulent and very illegal private gambling club was doing: he ignored the distant crump of falling bombs and roar of anti-aircraft batteries and concentrated on the game before him. So far that night he had won a satisfying sum from Ian Fleming.

'Well,' Brice said smugly when Fleming started dealing for the third time, 'your Washington friends told me to avoid playing with you. Now I see it was to prevent me from becoming overconfident.'

'Careful, Mr Brice,' Fleming said coolly. 'You're in grave danger of tempting me to use a devastating technique

I tried on the Germans in Lisbon. The idea was to win staggering sums from their embassy staff in order to cripple the Nazi war machine.'

Brice smiled. 'Did it work?'

A much closer bomb dislodged some plaster from the ceiling.

'It's just possible,' Fleming said drily without looking up, 'that His Majesty's Government paid for that bomb.'

Brice laughed, and then noticed a man in evening dress signalling their table. 'Does he want you or me?' Brice asked.

Fleming turned around. 'Me, I fancy. Excuse me, old boy.'

Brice watched the two men hold a whispered conference in the corner of the room near the doorway. Fleming returned a minute later, sat down, and picked up his cards. He gazed at them for a few seconds while Brice waited patiently.

'*U700* has arrived at the Vickers submarine works at Barrow-in-Furness,' said Fleming quietly. 'Engineers have just finished giving her a preliminary once-over. You'll never guess what they've found jammed in one of her bow torpedo tubes.'

Brice suddenly forgot the game.

'Not a magnetic . . .'

'Right first time,' Fleming cut in.

Brice whistled softly. 'Complete?'

'Complete. The engineers have managed to draw it back into the boat. They'll leave it in place until you've had a chance to examine it.'

'When?' Brice asked eagerly.

'Whenever you like, old boy. I've been told to take you to Barrow to make sure you see everything you want to see and take plenty of photographs for the Newport Torpedo Station's photograph album.'

111

Brice grinned. 'About time. Another month in England, and my wife might file for a divorce.'

Fleming frowned at his cards. 'The question is, old boy,' he said, fanning out his cards on the green baize, 'will you be able to afford the film?'

37

The main feature of No. 1 Prisoner of War Camp, Grizedale Hall, was the hall itself. It had panelled walls and an ornate vaulted ceiling. Along one wall were a line of windows that afforded a panoramic view of Lake Windermere sparkling in the September sunlight. The hall served as a mess hall for meals and a prisoners' common room at other times. Even after a week, Anders still found it hard to accept that he was in a prison camp. The sense of unreality was heightened when he stood at a window and gazed down the uninterrupted slope to the lakeside, for the main barbed wire fence was concealed by a fold in the ground. Even the watchtowers had been constructed to look like firewatchers' lookouts.

It was lunchtime. Kretschmer was sitting at the head table with Paul Faulk and Willi Leymann, a jovial Bavarian lawyer who had joined the Luftwaffe, obtained a commission as a captain, and had been in the first aircraft to be brought down by a barrage balloon. Anders felt Kretschmer's eyes on him as he waited in the line at the serving table.

'It's only a five hour walk to Barrow-in-Furness,' Leymann was saying. 'So if Schumann and Kirk have a sound escape plan, I don't think we ought to stand in their way.'

Kretschmer's eyes went to one of the trestle tables at the side of the hall where Schumann and Kirk were watching him. They were two brutish gunnery officers who had been picked out of the sea when the *Bismarck* went down. Since then they had been inseparable. They were giants, both over six feet tall – and certain to attract attention if they broke out successfully.

'No,' Kretschmer said firmly.

'We'll have to give them a reason,' Leymann pointed out.

'What do you know about Barrow?' inquired Kretschmer.

The rotund lawyer smiled. 'Kirk says it's a large port. He's certain there'll be regular sailings to Southern Ireland that they could stow away on.'

'It's a large port,' Kretschmer agreed. 'But it also happens to be the home of the largest submarine construction yard in the country. There would be dockyard police *and* military police and customs – and perhaps civilian police as well. They wouldn't get within two-hundred metres of a ship.'

Anders collected his meal and started toward his table at the back of the hall where Conrad Shulke was sitting.

'As much as I'd like to see those two thugs out of here,' said Kretschmer, 'they'll have to come up with something better than that if they want to stay together . . . Anders!'

Anders nearly dropped his tray when the voice cracked out behind him. Kretschmer was beckoning him over.

'Yes, commander?'

'How are you settling in?' Kretschmer asked pleasantly.

'Very well, thank you.'

'You're not finding my gardening schedules too hard, I hope?'

'No, commander. I like gardening.'

'Excellent.' Kretschmer nodded his head dismissively.

Anders returned to his table and sat down. Shulke noticed that the young naval officer was shaken.

'What's the matter?'

'Nothing.'

'What did Kretschmer want?'

'Is it your business?'

Schulke looked hurt. 'Sorry.'

'He wanted to know how I was coping with the gardening. Sorry I was rude, Conrad. Do you want my dinner? I'm not hungry.'

Under any other circumstances Shulke would have understood why Anders wasn't hungry; the dish was what the British referred to by the disturbing name of shepherd's pie: mashed potato flecked with almost invisible specks of what everyone presumed and hoped was minced meat. But Anders' refusal to eat his meals was becoming a common occurrence.

'Do you want to talk about it?'

'Talk about what?'

Shulke shrugged. 'Not eating. Not sleeping.'

'Who said I wasn't sleeping?' Anders demanded irritably.

Shulke speared one of Anders' carrots and popped it in his mouth. 'There's two types of breathing at night: wide-awake breathing and sound-asleep breathing. Yours is wide-awake breathing.'

'What's it to you?'

'Curious.' He paused. 'No, I'm worried about you.'

'There's nothing to be worried about.'

'Fine. So eat.'

Anders spooned up some mashed potato and thrust it into his mouth. Shulke gave him an encouraging smile and was repaid with a scowl.

* * *

That night, when the prisoners in the dormitory were asleep and snoring, Shulke sensed that someone was standing by his bed. He groped for his matches and saw it was Anders, staring down at him. Shulke knew from the young U-boat officer's expression that something was desperately wrong. He let the match go out and said quietly, 'What's wrong, Bernard?'

There was a long silence. When Anders finally spoke, his voice was a distraught whisper in the darkness.

'I'm sorry to disturb you, Conrad.'

'Yes?' Shulke prompted, lifting himself on to an elbow.

There was a pause, then, 'You were shot down.'

'Yes,' Shulke said, baffled. 'A reconnaissance flight over the Channel. Did you wake me up to ask that?'

'Do you think the others will learn about *how* you were shot down?'

'What others?'

'Kretschmer. Faulk. The whole camp.'

'I don't understand what you mean,' Shulke said with poorly disguised annoyance. 'I've told everyone what happened.'

'I mean the exact details,' Anders persisted. 'Your position. The time. The type of boat that picked you up. Do you think they could ever find out that sort of thing?'

Shulke was puzzled. 'Well I suppose they could if they wanted to. Why?' There was no answer. 'Bernard?'

'Yes.'

'I'm a good listener if you want to talk.'

'No,' Anders said quietly. 'It doesn't matter. I'm sorry I woke you.'

Shulke reached a hand out into the darkness, but Anders had gone back to his bed.

38

Two days later at Lorient, Doenitz's Mercedes pulled up outside the hangar where the Junkers was kept. Doenitz and Kneller approached the door set into the main door and were, to Doenitz's delight, challenged by a military policeman. The admiral had ordered a strict security clamp down on the hangar and was pleased to discover that his instructions were being scrupulously obeyed.

A minute later they were inside the hangar surveying the trusty old Ju52. Mechanics were noisily stripping fittings from the aircraft's cabin and carrying them to Goder, who was weighing them on an industrial beam balance and transferring the figures to a blackboard.

It was some seconds before Goder noticed his visitors. He quickly gave Doenitz a clumsy salute, which Doenitz waved aside.

'Just so long as you're getting on with the job, Goder. That's all that matters. How is it coming along?'

'Better than I thought, admiral. It's amazing how much of this Iron Annie we can manage without.'

'How much weight has she shed?' Doenitz asked.

Goder turned to the blackboard. 'I haven't totalled it yet, admiral. But I would guess the best part of a ton of nonessential equipment.' The pilot grinned. 'Tomorrow we start on the essential equipment.'

Kneller frowned at Goder's temerity, but Doenitz merely smiled.

'The torpedo arrived an hour ago,' Goder said, pointing to a long, graceful weapon resting on a trolley. 'The dockyard has promised to have the release gear finished by Tuesday.'

Doenitz examined the torpedo with an expert eye. It was a Type G7e fitted with a magnetic warhead – the weapon that Doenitz was convinced would win the war for Germany if only the OKM would stop interfering in his management of the U-boat offensive. They had even refused to allow U-boat commanders to defend themselves against warships of the neutral United States, which were now harassing U-boats with ever increasing vigour.

'There is one thing, admiral,' Goder said. 'The torpedo is heavier than I thought.'

Doenitz nodded. 'This one has the Wotan armoured warhead, Goder. I'll tell the Torpedo Establishment to send you a G7a. They're a hundred kilos lighter. Not so powerful but powerful enough to destroy a U-boat.'

39

'Look out!' Shulke yelled.

Lillian's station wagon swerved violently, brakes screeching and tyres spewing gravel. Shulke grabbed Anders' sleeve and hauled him backward but he was too late. The vehicle's radiator clipped the garden rake Anders was carrying and spun him around. Before he could recover his balance, the station wagon's side mirror smacked into his ribs and threw him to the ground.

Lillian jumped from the driver's seat while the vehicle rolled to a standstill. 'Don't move him!' she called out to Shulke. But Anders had moved himself; he was sitting up and looking aggrieved by the time Lillian knelt beside him.

'I'm terribly sorry,' Lillian said. 'Those stupid brakes. It was my fault. Are you all right?'

A crowd of prisoners was gathering, offering suggestions.

'Yes, I think so,' Anders said, reaching a cautious hand behind his back. He winced in pain.

'I'd better have a look at him,' Lillian said. She noticed that Anders had allowed his eyes to linger on her legs and guessed that there was nothing seriously wrong with him. 'Help me get him to the sick bay.'

'Nothing to worry about,' Lillian said cheerfully to Anders who was stretched out naked on his stomach. 'Just a rather nasty bruise, which I'm terribly sorry about. Okay, you can get dressed.'

Anders climbed off the couch gingerly and self-consciously turned away from Lillian as he pulled up his trousers.

Lillian noticed how thin and pale he was. He was not merely thin – he was emaciated.

'The bruise is the same shape as my car mirror,' she said smiling.

'So?' Anders said as he pulled on his shirt.

'You've lost weight.'

'It's the food,' was Anders' noncommittal reply. He turned and noticed the newspaper lying on Lillian's desk. It was partly covered by a magazine, but the two-inch-high headlines were clearly visible.

The British press had been given the *U700* story.

Suddenly it was too much. The room began to spin madly. Anders felt as if his head had been wrenched from his body. Superheated steam was roaring in his ears.

And then there was a total and merciful silence.

*　　*　　*

At that moment Willi Leymann was about to check Paul Faulk's king with a rook.

But he never completed the move. A newspaper landed on the homemade chessboard, scattering the carefully carved pieces on the floor. The two players looked angrily up at Schumann and Kirk who were towering over them, grim-faced and silent.

'Read,' Kirk said economically, jabbing a huge finger at the newspaper.

There was no need for the chess players to ask which news item the giant gunnery officer was referring to. There was only one, and it was emblazoned across the frontpage in two-inch headlines: U-BOAT SURRENDERS WITHOUT FIGHT!

Lillian closed the sickbay window so that the work crew clipping the lawn could not hear what she had to say. She had long discovered that the prisoners had developed a taste for gossip. She turned from the window and looked thoughtfully at Anders who was sitting up and sipping from a glass of water. She picked up his medical card and tapped it against her teeth.

'Have you been passing blood, Lieutenant Anders?'

'Why?'

'I thought that you might have an ulcer.'

'Why should you think that?'

'Get on the scales please.'

'You weighed me less than a month ago – when I first arrived.'

'Well now I'm going to weigh you again,' Lillian answered irritably. 'On the scales please.'

Anders put the glass down and stepped on to the weighing machine.

'All right. Now show me your nails please.'

Anders held his hands out for inspection, catching a faint whiff of perfume.

Lillian regarded Anders steadily. 'Okay,' she said. 'Why aren't you eating your food?'

'How do you know I'm not?' Anders countered.

'Vitamin deficiency. You have every symptom plus an eleven pound weight loss since you arrived. I want to know why.'

'I don't like the food.'

Lillian flushed angrily. 'There's nothing wrong with the food here. You're getting fresh vegetables that a lot of people in this country would be glad to have. There's not much meat but that's something you can blame on your U-boat comrades. My medical cards are inspected by the Red Cross. Major Veitch would be very angry if they got the impression that we're ill-treating prisoners-of-war. So do you tell me why you're not eating properly, or do I recommend your transfer to another camp?'

From where Anders was sitting, he could see through the sickbay window. He noticed two men walking across the lawn. One was the unmistakable stocky figure of Leymann. The other looked like Faulk. They were both examining a newspaper.

'Maybe a transfer isn't such a bad idea,' Anders said dispiritedly.

Lillian was surprised. There had been no bullying incidents at the camp since Kretschmer had arrived, but Major Veitch had warned his staff to remain on the alert.

'Why?'

Anders saw Kretschmer join Leymann and Faulk.

'You wouldn't understand,' Anders said. 'What do you know about war?'

Lillian looked at him long and hard. 'I was among a party of army nurses evacuated from Dunkirk last year,' she said evenly. 'My sister was a nurse too. She was in charge of a group of officers' children being taken to

Canada last Christmas when her ship was torpedoed by a U-boat. She later died of exposure in the lifeboat.'

Anders pulled his eyes away from the three men in the garden.

Lillian forced a smile. 'I've never mentioned this to anyone in here. One of the little girls who survived said that the U-boat had a golden horseshoe on the conning tower.'

A prisoner who had helped carry Anders to the sickbay was pointing out his whereabouts to the three men on the lawn. It didn't need much imagination on Anders' part to guess what was being said.

'Have you told him?' he asked.

Lillian shook her head. 'What would be the point?' Anders noticed that Faulk was walking with long, purposeful strides toward the hall.

Lillian smiled. 'Well now I've told you my little secret . . .' She looked expectantly at Anders.

Faulk had disappeared from sight. He'd now be in the front hall, thought Anders. Turning left . . .

'I was the first officer on a new U-boat,' Anders began hesitantly.

'What was its number, or is that something you're not allowed to mention?'

Faulk would now be striding down the corridor toward the sickbay. Bernard thought he could hear footsteps approaching.

'It was U . . .'

He got no further. There was a loud, determined hammering on the door, and then it opened. Faulk stood in the doorway. A lock of hair had fallen across the clean-cut features.

'I'm terribly sorry to intrude, nurse, but we've just heard about the accident and we are all wondering if Lieutenant Anders is all right.'

121

Lillian noticed that he didn't look at Anders as he spoke.

'He'll be fine,' Lillian said. 'A nasty bruise, which is all my fault, but it'll clear up in a few days.'

Faulk gave a little bow. His courtly manners did much to dispel Lillian's initial annoyance at the way he had burst into her sickbay.

'We are all very concerned for him,' Faulk continued. 'The commander would be grateful to see Lieutenant Anders as soon as possible.'

'There's no reason why he shouldn't go now,' Lillian replied. She suddenly realized that they were talking about Anders as if he were not in the room.

Kretschmer lit another cheroot and tossed the matches on his desk. He drew on the slim cigar and watched Anders through the smoke. He noticed that the young naval officer's gaze was fixed on the pile of newspapers that Leymann had placed on his desk.

Kretschmer nodded to Leymann. The portly little Bavarian picked up the top paper and read aloud from the frontpage:

'Squadron Leader Thompson, the pilot of the Hudson which captured *U700*, said that the white surrender flag waved from the conning tower was the biggest shock of his life. "I expected the U-boat to dive or open fire with its anti-aircraft guns," he told reporters. "The last thing I expected it to do was surrender – especially as the U-boat appeared to be undamaged by the depth charges we had dropped."'

Anders was about to speak, but Kretschmer held up his finger for silence.

'An admiralty spokesman refused to comment on *U700*'s future,' Leymann continued, 'but said that the capture of an *intact* U-boat was of major importance and that the possibility of it serving under the White Ensign could not be ruled out.'

There was a long silence. It was even possible to hear Kretschmer's watch ticking.

'What about the other papers?' Kretschmer asked.

'They all carry the same story, commander. Virtually word for word.'

'And they all refer to an *intact* U-boat?'

'Yes, commander.'

'They're all lying!' Anders said suddenly. 'The depth charges caused extensive damage. The boat was thrown on its side. And we *did* open fire!'

Kretschmer addressed Anders for the first time. 'Why didn't you dive?'

'One of the hydroplanes was jammed.'

'Which one?' Kretschmer snapped. 'Bow? Stern? Port? Starboard?'

'I don't know,' Anders said miserably. 'But the boat *was* damaged. Commander Weiner saw the Hudson coming in for another attack. We were helpless. He had no choice but to surrender.'

'U-boats have scuttling charges, do they not, Anders?'

'Yes.'

'Why weren't they detonated?'

'I don't remember,' Anders said ineffectually. 'I think the wiring had been damaged by the depth charges.'

Kretschmer looked contemptuous. 'All right, Anders. Wait outside.'

'The boat *was* damaged,' Anders repeated defiantly.

'Wait outside.' Kretschmer's voice was emotionless.

Anders saluted and left the room. Kretschmer raised an inquiring eyebrow at Leymann.

'I think he's telling the truth,' the plump lawyer said.

'You're the expert,' Kretschmer said evenly.

'Meaning you don't believe him?'

Kretschmer thought for a moment. 'I'm not sure, Willi.'

'You've got to consider that the British might be putting out a false story to create unrest in the U-boat arm,' Leymann pointed out.

Kretschmer summoned Anders back into the office. 'I've decided to give you the benefit of the doubt, Anders.'

A weight seemed to be lifted from Anders' shoulders. 'Thank you, commander.'

'You may go.'

Anders turned to leave.

'One thing, Anders.' Kretschmer gestured to the news-papers. 'If those reports *are* telling the truth, you will most likely be hanged for cowardice after the war.'

Lillian returned Anders' medical card to the drawer and tidied up the sickbay. She decided to make herself a cup of tea, and while she was waiting for the kettle to boil, she picked up her paper and read the lead story on the front page.

40

That night, some 400 miles to the south-west in Southern Ireland, Patrick Gallagher was sitting in Toomley's drinking his third pint of the evening. He was careful with his money – to be seen out drinking every night would start gossip and speculation, and that would never do. On the other hand, he could buy the lads the occasional round because he was unmarried and his official job as a tele-grapher was well-paid. It was all a matter of balance.

A man who was not a regular entered the bar and hoisted

himself onto one of the two stools that Toomley provided for those customers who didn't understand that bars should be leaned on and not sat at. Gallagher watched him out of the corner of his eye. He was about forty, short, and a little overweight. He was wearing a light blue suit. He ordered a whiskey and asked Toomley if he had any cigars. Toomley sold him the ancient Havana that had been in the sweet jar behind the bar for as long as Gallagher could remember.

The stranger lit the cigar, inhaled deeply, then looked suspiciously at the glowing tip. He caught Gallagher's eye, smiled, and raised his glass.

'Nice evening for fishing,' he said.

Gallagher was about to point out that it was pouring with rain when a warning bell jangled at the back of his mind. He lowered his tankard and stared at the stranger in the etched mirror at the back of the bar.

'Of course,' the stranger continued, 'I once tried fresh-water fishing, but I didn't like the taste of anything I caught. Now I stick to sea fishing.'

Gallagher turned. The stranger had been word-perfect. With a sinking heart Gallagher realized he was going to start earning all the money that had been paid into his Dublin account.

41

Five days later in Lorient, a truck drew up outside the hangar where Admiral Doenitz's Ju52 was being prepared for its mission.

Two fitters dragged back the tarpaulins and passed a heavy lifting chain around the torpedo. A mobile crane lifted the weapon onto a trolley. Five minutes later, with much armwaving and shouted instructions from Goder, the torpedo's centre-of-gravity marks were being positioned under the open claws of the makeshift release mechanism that had been attached to the underside of the Ju52's fuselage.

Satisfied that the torpedo was correctly positioned, Goder banged the side of the fuselage with his fist. Hartz, sitting in the copilot's seat, operated the lever that had been installed between the two seats.

The heavy steel claws snapped shut around the torpedo's fat body. Goder was delighted and signalled twice with his fist on the fuselage. The claws opened. Goder measured the distance across the open jaws of the clamps with a pair of large calipers and was about to make some adjustments to the setting screws, when he noticed two pairs of immaculately polished shoes and two pairs of faultlessly pressed trousers standing nearby.

'Good morning, Goder,' Doenitz said as the naval pilot scrambled out from under the fuselage. 'How's everything going?'

'Like a dream, admiral,' Goder said, wiping his hands on a rag. He pointed to the torpedo. 'It fits beautifully, but I think we'll have to rivet extra stiffeners to the outside of the fuselage around the mounting points to prevent flexing. That's in case we get buffeted by bad weather and can't get above it. She's not designed to have a ton weight hanging from her.'

Doenitz smiled. Goder was enjoying himself, and people who enjoyed their work invariably did it well.

'Will it fly properly?' Kneller asked.

Goder's expression became solemn. 'Fly – yes. Properly – no.'

Doenitz needed all his self-control to keep from laughing.

Kneller did not share Doenitz's amusement. 'So it won't be airworthy?'

Goder looked shocked. 'Good heavens, no. We've cut holes in the bulkheads so big they frighten me, but it will fly. There is one thing that's worrying Hartz and me. We've been going over the maps of the Barrow area until we know every inlet and creek. There's a thousand and one places the British could anchor the U-boat. We won't have the fuel for a long search. We're going to have to fly straight to it.'

'That problem has been anticipated,' Doenitz said. 'You'll be given *U700*'s exact position before you leave.'

Goder looked astonished. He knew no reconnaissance aircraft flew that far north, and even if they did, the Luftwaffe was not likely to provide the Kreigsmarine with information.

'How will you get the U-boat's position, admiral?'

Doenitz's expression hardened. 'You ask too many questions, Goder. Carry on with your work.'

Goder saluted and crawled back under the Ju52's fuselage.

'He's impertinent,' Kneller commented.

Doenitz gestured to the tangled pile of fixtures and fittings that had been removed from the Junkers' interior. There were seats, a chemical toilet, the folding steps, several crates of small items and large pieces of aluminum floor section with jagged edges where they had been hacked away from the fuselage. Each item was labelled with its weight.

'He's efficient, John. He does his job well, and that's all I ask. I've given the grand admiral a firm promise that *U700* will be destroyed – a promise that he's conveyed to Hitler.'

Kneller said nothing as they walked to the door. He had

heard that Hitler nearly had an apoplectic fit when he had learned about *U700*'s surrender.

'This observer the OKM are sending to Barrow,' Doenitz said. 'Is he ready yet?'

'He's on his way, admiral.'

Doenitz nodded with satisfaction. 'What was the hold up?'

'His radio transmitter. He wasn't happy about it. Barrow is virtually hemmed in by the Cumberland Fells, which means that it has to be extra-powerful to get a signal out. He also needs a thirty-metre-high antenna. It all makes for extra bulk, which the observer is most unhappy about.'

'What's his name?' Doenitz asked disinterestedly. 'Gallagher,' Kneller replied. 'Patrick Arthur Gallagher.'

42

'Patrick Arthur Gallagher,' he said in his best Belfast accent to the Liverpool Docks police officer.

'Your identity card please.'

'Sure thing.' Gallagher eased his motorcycle backward on to its stand. Two other policemen took over the inspection of passengers disembarking from the ship so that there wasn't a hold up.

The policeman carefully inspected Gallagher's identity card and seemed satisfied. There was no reason why he shouldn't be – the simple document, although a forger's delight, was genuine.

The policeman returned the card and looked curiously at Gallagher's Douglas. The panniers were crammed; there was a packed tent and sleeping bag lashed across the pillion and several fishing rod sleeves tied to the side of the machine.

'A fishing holiday,' Gallagher explained in response to the policeman's polite question.

A minute later he was wheeling his motorcycle toward the customs shed where the rest of the passengers from the ship were forming a line.

'Good morning, sir,' a voice said.

Gallagher stopped and turned. A senior customs officer was smiling pleasantly at him. He pointed to a pair of double doors at the rear of the customs shed. 'Perhaps you'd be kind enough to take your bike through those doors please, sir.'

Gallagher remained outwardly calm and smiling. He pointed at the line. 'Now I was thinking that that was the queue for customs.'

'It is, sir,' the uniformed officer said. 'But it's a little crowded in there. If you'd be good enough to follow me please . . .'

Gallagher's spirits fell even further as he pushed his machine into what could only be described as a workshop. There was a bench against a wall that was festooned with wrenches, pliers, and screwdrivers hanging from rusty nails. Near the double doors was a vehicle inspection pit equipped with two powerful swivelling lights. In the middle of the workshop was a low industrial table – the sort that an engine could be placed on for dismantling. Two men in overalls were sipping from chipped mugs. A third in uniform was warming his hands over an evil-smelling oil heater. He looked up and smiled as Gallagher entered.

'Ah, good morning, sir. Prop your bike against the table. Would you like a mug of cocoa while you're waiting?'

Gallagher noticed that he could talk and smile at the same time. Maybe he practised in front of a mirror. Gallagher showed him that he could do the same trick.

'Do you want to look in my suitcase then?'

The customs officer kept smiling. 'More than that, sir. More than that. Maybe you'd help us out a bit by unpacking everything and spreading it out on that table?'

'Even my tent and sleeping bag?'

'Everything, sir. Everything. Might as well be hanged for a sheep as for a lamb, eh?'

Gallagher bent over his motorcycle to unbuckle the pannier straps and wondered if the three men could hear his heart pounding.

43

The speedometer needle was hovering at the hundred mark as the grey, supercharged, 4½-litre 1930 Bentley coupé screamed north-west along the ten-mile straightaway on the A5 between Bletchley and Towcester.

Brice had a red-blooded American's love of speed, but there was something indecent about thrashing along at a hundred miles an hour in a huge, open-topped machine that was built like and looked like a customized tractor. At least Fleming seemed able to handle the monster. In fact, Brice admitted to himself, Fleming was an excellent driver; he was relaxed, sitting well back in the driver's seat, arms straight, hands on the wheel at the correct ten-minutes-to-two position.

'I didn't know you had roads as straight as this!' Brice yelled. Normal conversation was impossible: everything had to be shouted above the roar of the wind and the ear-splitting howl of the anguished supercharger.

'Roman,' Fleming answered. 'The only Europeans who knew how to build roads until the Germans came along.'

'When do we get to Barrow?'

'Late this afternoon, old boy. Fancy a spell of driving?'

'On the wrong side of the road? No thanks.'

Fleming laughed. 'The only reason I'm clipping along like this is to make you feel at home.'

Brice said nothing; the speedometer needle was edging up to a hundred and ten. He hoped that it wasn't a straight road all the way to Barrow-in-Furness. His nerves couldn't stand it.

44

Even Gallagher was surprised at just how much he had been able to pack into his motorcycle panniers. There was so much clothing, camping equipment and fishing tackle strewn across the table that it didn't seem possible it could all be restowed.

The three customs men had literally taken everything apart. They had even shined a torch inside his Primus stove and opened up all his tins containing sinkers and hooks.

The smiling customs officer picked up a reel and drew out a yard of line. He tried to break it and couldn't.

'Heavy line, sir.'

Gallagher grinned. 'I thought I might try for a spot of mackerel. Are you a fishing man, sir?'

The customs officer unscrewed the top of a jar of Brylcreem and probed the contents with a finger. 'No, sir. I thought you had good fishing in Ireland?'

'It is that,' Gallagher agreed. 'But when you've only a few days' holiday a year, you like to be spending it on a challenge.'

One of the overall-clad customs men was peering in

the motorcycle's petrol tank. He sniffed and seemed disappointed to discover that it contained petrol.

'You won't believe this,' Gallagher said cheerfully, 'but I once caught a fresh-water cod that long.' He spread out his hands.

The smiling customs officer entered into the spirit of the game. 'An Irish fresh-water cod was it, sir?'

'Well of course. Didn't it hop up on the bank beside me and guzzle me whole pot o' Guinness?'

The three customs men laughed.

An hour later Gallagher was riding through Liverpool. He was seething inwardly at his cavalier treatment by the customs men. The arrogant bastards hadn't even helped him repack his gear. Mother of God, how he loathed the British and everything they stood for.

There was one consolation he savoured as he rode through the dockland streets: at least the Luftwaffe had given the place a good plastering.

He began to sing his favourite tune. No one would hear it above the roar of the motorcycle engine: *'We're marching to war against England!'*

45

By late afternoon the grey Bentley coupé was north of Liverpool and skirting the breath-taking sweep of Morecambe Bay. The sea was a distant ribbon of light on the horizon.

'The tide comes in faster than a man can run,' Fleming said. 'The stagecoaches used to take short cuts across the sands to get to Barrow. Quite a number of people drowned over the years.'

Brice looked at the map. Another 45 minutes and they'd be in Barrow. The town was on the edge of the Lake District, and the scenery was incredibly beautiful. As he mentioned to Fleming, it was hard to believe that the north of England was fighting the same war as the south.

'We'll drive through Liverpool on the way back,' Fleming promised.

Brice forgot the map and relaxed to enjoy the last few miles of the long drive. He guessed that Fleming was tired; the Bentley was cruising at a steady forty, it's 4½-litre engine burbling contentedly under the eight feet of hood.

A horn suddenly blasted immediately behind Brice. He turned. A girl driving an ancient station wagon was sitting on Fleming's tail. She sounded her horn again and tried to pass the Bentley but was forced back by an oncoming truck. Brice smiled at her, but her face remained fixed in a frown of concentration. She was wearing what looked like a nurse's uniform. A pretty kid. She sounded her horn repeatedly.

'The most dangerous thing about living in London,' Fleming said as his foot went down on the throttle pedal, 'isn't the bombs but the ATS girls driving ambulances.'

Brice's laugh was snatched away by the wind as the giant car surged effortlessly into the eighties.

Gallagher was singing at the top of his voice as he bowled along at fifty miles an hour. The motorcycle's finely tuned engine was running like a sewing machine, the late evening sun felt pleasantly warm on his back, and all was right with the world. He was just thinking that it would soon be time to look for a suitable camp site when he thought he heard the distinctive whine of a supercharged engine. He glanced over his shoulder, and the two staring King of the Road Lucas headlamps on either side of a howling supercharger were suddenly upon him. He yanked the handlebars to the left and skidded the Douglas safely onto the shoulder, catching a glimpse of the driver before being blinded by the dense cloud of swirling dust in the charging monster's wake: wavy RNVR stripes on his sleeve, an English officer, relaxed, confident and uncaring – just like the bastard who, in September 1920 at Balbriggan, near Dublin, had ordered the despised Black and Tans to open fire on the crowd. Afterwards, Gallagher's father had been found bleeding slowly to death on the cobblestones.

Gallagher was about to restart the Douglas's engine when a station wagon driven by a nurse came hurtling past, missing him by inches. He sighed. He was beginning to realize that danger in the spying business could come from unexpected quarters.

46

It was sunset as Lillian drove through the stableyard and parked outside Grizedale Hall. The few prisoners strolling along the gravelled drive gave mock screams of terror when they saw her and made a great show of diving for safety. Lillian wasn't particularly amused. She was concerned about the station wagon's overheated engine; the straining radiator cap was blowing out enough steam to sterilize a hospital. Perhaps trying to chase the Bentley had been a mistake, but she couldn't stand men who drove as if they owned the road.

She looked quickly around to see if any prisoners were watching before clicking the hidden switch under the dashboard that isolated the vehicle's ignition. Her father had fitted it for her. It was less messy than removing the rotor arm every time she left the station wagon unattended. She locked the door and was about to enter the hall when she noticed Anders pushing a wheelbarrow.

'Good evening, Bernard. How's the bruise?'

Anders set his wheelbarrow down. 'It's fading I think.'

Lillian nodded and then looked anxiously at the steaming radiator cap. 'I've never known it to do that before. Do you suppose it's all right?'

She was about to touch the cap, but Anders stopped her. 'It's best to let it cool down first, then see if it needs more water.'

Lillian smiled. 'I know nothing about cars. So long as they go, the faster the better.'

'You like going fast?'

Lillian looked up quickly to see if the young naval officer was teasing her, but his eyes were serious. Anders, she suspected, did not have a strong sense of humour.

'If you like going fast,' Anders continued, 'it is important to have good brakes. Is your handbrake on?'

'Yes. Hard on.'

Anders gave the vehicle a gentle push. It rolled a yard.

'Perhaps your brakes need attention?' Anders suggested. 'Relining?'

'That's what the garage in Barrow said. But they can't look at them for a month. It's getting impossible to get anything done these days.'

An army truck passed the station wagon and pulled up twenty yards away, outside the front entrance to the hall.

'I could do them for you if you got the linings from the garage,' Anders offered.

Lillian chuckled. 'It's funny when you think about it. I nearly run you over, and so you offer to repair my brakes.' She watched the new arrival over Anders' shoulder. One of the guards was helping him down from the tailboard because his left arm was in a wrist sling.

135

'Will the commandant mind?' Anders asked.

'He didn't mind Lieutenant Faulk looking at them,' Lillian said. She was amazed that the new prisoner could look so smart after a ten-hour train journey. His naval uniform looked as if it had just been pressed and his collar was spotless. He waved aside the guard's offer of further help and swung his kitbag on to his shoulder with his free hand. As he straightened, Lillian noticed a bold scar that traversed his left cheek. 'New arrival,' she commented to Anders. 'Another navy type.'

Anders tuned around, and in that moment his legs felt as if they had suddenly dissolved. The new arrival was smiling at him. It was not a smile of friendship but one of triumph.

'My God,' Anders whispered. 'Stein.'

Thirty minutes later, Anders was waiting in the corridor outside Kretschmer's office. Stein hadn't wasted any time, he reflected bitterly. He could hear voices. Angry voices. The door opened, and Faulk beckoned.

'You can come in now.'

Stein was standing in front of Kretschmer's desk. Leymann was by the window, and Kretschmer was sitting with his chair tilted back, smoking a cheroot. Anders heard the door close softly behind him.

'Lieutenant Stein has made a very serious allegation about the loss of *U700*,' Kretschmer said without preamble. 'He says the newspapers are telling the truth – that it surrendered without a fight and that you played a significant role in its surrender. Is that true?'

'No,' Anders said. 'I wasn't even on the bridge when Weiner surrendered. But Stein was.'

Kretschmer's expressionless eyes turned to Stein. 'Is that true?'

'Yes,' Stein said. He indicated his wounded arm. 'I

got this offering the only resistance that *U700* put up. Immediately after I was taken below, I circulated a petition in which every member of the crew pledged support for Lieutenant Anders if he arrested Weiner and countermanded the surrender.'

'And I went on to the bridge to arrest the captain,' Anders protested. 'But it was too late because an armed trawler had arrived.'

'He had no intention of arresting Weiner,' Stein sneered. 'I don't suppose he even had the guts to take my Luger out of his pocket.'

'All right,' Kretschmer broke in before Anders had time to protest.

Anders and Stein remained silent while Kretschmer drew slowly on his cheroot. Then the U-boat ace fastened his hypnotic eyes on Anders. 'Weiner paddled across to the destroyer in one of the U-boat's dinghies?'

'Yes, commander,' Anders replied. 'He didn't want to. He wanted to be the last to leave the U-boat so that he could open the main vents and detonate the scuttling charges after the crew was safe.'

'He was ordered to paddle to the destroyer?'

'Yes. They said that they would sink us if he didn't.' Anders looked up, hoping for a flicker of understanding in Kretschmer's eyes, and found none.

'So you were left in command of the U-boat,' Kretschmer stated.

'No, commander.'

Kretschmer raised an eyebrow 'You were *U700*'s first officer, were you not?'

'Yes,' said Anders. 'But as we had surrendered, command of the boat had been transferred to the captain of the British destroyer – even though he wasn't on board.'

Kretschmer's tone was suddenly icy. 'You were left in

137

command of *U700*, and you didn't order the boat to fight, and you didn't take the necessary steps to ensure the boat was scuttled?'

'I gave the order to scuttle the boat,' Stein said.

'And I cancelled it!' Anders retorted.

'Why?' Kretschmer demanded.

'Because we couldn't abandon the boat first,' Anders answered. 'The destroyer had threatened to open fire if any of the crew appeared on the deck before they could get a boarding party to us. I didn't want any needless killing.'

'Didn't it occur to you that the destroyer wanted to make sure that you didn't scuttle?' Kretschmer asked.

Anders made no reply.

'Commander,' Stein said, 'it's clearly stated in Battle Orders . . .'

'Thank you, Stein,' Kretschmer cut in sharply, 'but I do know what's in the Battle Orders.' He stared at the two naval officers for some seconds and stubbed out his cheroot in the cocoa tin lid that served as an ashtray. 'All right, you two – you can go. Show Stein his quarters please, Faulk.'

Stein looked surprised. 'But surely, commander, you're not going to let this little coward . . .'

'When I've decided what to do, Stein,' Kretschmer interrupted harshly, 'I'll let you know.'

Kretschmer waited until he and Leymann were alone before he lit another cheroot, blowing a thin cloud of smoke at the ceiling.

'What are you thinking, Willi?'

'I'm thinking that Stein is going to make trouble,' said the tubby lawyer. 'What little I've seen of him is enough. He's the sort to gravitate toward types like Schumann and Kirk, and when he does . . .' Leymann left the sentence unfinished.

'There will be no bullying in this camp,' Kretschmer said firmly.

'How will you stop it? As I see it, you're going to have to ask Major Veitch to have Anders transferred to another camp.'

'Pass the problem on to someone else?' Kretschmer sat forward. 'Listen, Willi. A U-boat has a crew of over forty. There's a good chance that there'd be one or two at any camp Anders is sent to. That's assuming that I ask Major Veitch to transfer him – which I won't.'

Leymann sighed. 'Which means that you're going to have to protect Anders, which means that some of the army and Luftwaffe types will be accusing you of favouritism toward a fellow U-boat officer. Which means that there will be trouble – real trouble – and we'll all end up at camps run by the Poles.'

Kretschmer inhaled deeply on his cigar. Leymann was right – protecting Anders from mob violence was going to be difficult. He had no sympathy for a coward – if indeed, Anders was guilty of cowardice. But that would be something for a court-martial to decide after the war. In the meantime, it was his duty to see that Anders came to no harm without alienating the respect that the POWs had for their senior officer. It was, Kretschmer reflected, a seemingly insurmountable problem. But there was a solution – a British solution – one that he remembered from his days as a student at Exeter. It was an unpleasant solution but it might work.

Kretschmer relit his cigar. 'There is a third course, Willi.'

47

It was dusk that evening when Gallagher found a suitable site on the Cumberland fells for his first transmission. It was a lonely spot by a stream that was sheltered by a tall, overhanging oak. The gasoline gauge on the motorcycle's instrument panel was indicating half full; that meant that he was over 600 feet above sea level. The gasoline gauge, like so much on the Douglas motorcycle, was not what it seemed.

Gallagher wheeled his machine to within three yards of the stream's bank and lifted it on to its stand. A minute later, he had unpacked all his fishing tackle and had the various tins and boxes spread out on the grass. He quickly assembled a fishing rod and loaded it with the reel containing the heavy line that the Liverpool customs officer had tried to break. A heavy lead sinker was attached to the free end of the line. He squinted up at the topmost branches of the oak tree and drew off about 100 feet of line from the reel. It was a good cast: the lead sinker, towing the line, which was in fact an insulated antenna wire, sailed up toward the top of the oak and became entangled in the upper branches.

The next stage of the operation was to get the transmitter-receiver working. Two grubby pieces of wire from the motorcycle's toolbox were quickly twisted around the two terminals intended for additional lighting when the machine was fitted with a sidecar. It was a simple matter for the other ends of the wires to be plugged into the tiny holes in one of the spare fishing line reels. Finally, Gallagher connected the end of the antenna wire to one of the spare terminals on the Douglas' magneto.

Everything was ready but there was still one minor, but important task to perform: he baited a real fishing line and cast it into the stream. He watched the float bob out into midstream.

He looked at his watch. It was five minutes to the hour.

At two minutes to the hour, he sat down on his folding stool beside the motorcycle, lifted the wired-up reel to his ear, and turned the Douglas' headlight switch to the left. Current started flowing from the machine's battery through the tiny radio valves sealed within the speedometer housing. It took a minute for them to warm up sufficiently to generate a gentle hum in the reel head phone that he held to his ear.

At thirty seconds to the hour, Gallagher rested his fingers lightly on the motorcycle's horn button. He stared at the second hand on his watch jerking toward the hour. When the hand reached '12' he rapidly tapped his call sign on the horn button. The impulses raced up the antenna wire and burst southward over England and across the Channel. They were picked up by receivers on the Eiffel Tower, re-amplified and beamed south-west to the receiving station at Lorient.

In the U-boat operations room, there was a sudden relaxing of tension as Gallagher's signals were decoded and clattered out on the cipher machine. Kneller gave a toothy smile; Admiral Doenitz remained impassive.

'Five-eight-one sent on four-eight decimal one,' the cipher clerk said, reading off the information that had appeared on the recording paper.

'That's him,' Kneller said. 'Acknowledge.'

Gallagher grinned to himself when he heard Lorient's faint bleeps in his headphone. His supple fingers went to the horn button again, and he began transmitting at high

141

speed. He was so fast that the wire recorder had to be switched on at Lorient to be certain of receiving the complete message.

Fifty miles south of Gallagher's campsite, Corporal Anderson of the Royal Army Corps of Signals was half-dozing in a wireless truck while his captain boredly leafed through a book. One of the radio receivers in front of Corporal Anderson was automatically sweeping the section of the shortwave band that had been allocated to the wireless truck for that evening. One by one, in a pattern of unceasing monotony, the stations of Europe would rise to a crescendo in the corporal's headphones and gradually fade to be replaced by the next station.

Oslo – a news bulletin; London – someone yakking away in German; Cologne – Wagner, it was always Wagner; London again – this time in French. Another twenty stations and then the whole boring cycle was repeated: Oslo –

Corporal Anderson was suddenly alert. He cut the automatic bandsweep on the receiver and reached up to crank the handwheel that turned the direction-finder loop on the truck's roof.

'Something, sir,' he said crisply.

The captain dropped his book and plugged his headphones in to the console.

'Some joker on forty-eight point one – just below Oslo,' Anderson continued. He stopped cranking when the needle on the meter before him dipped. 'Bearing three-three one.'

Using a protractor, the captain marked off a thick black line on a map of northern England. 'What's his reciprocal, corporal?'

'North, sir. Christ, he's fast.' Anderson tried to scribble

142

Gallagher's morse down, but it was impossible to keep up with the rapid stream of bleeps in his headphones.

'Ground wave or sky wave?' the captain asked.

'Definitely ground wave, sir. He's on our doorstep. That's the lot – he's stopped.'

The captain looked disappointed. There hadn't been time to call up C for Charlie to get a triangulation fix. He looked at the line he had slashed across the map. It ran off the coast at Barrow-in-Furness. Whoever the mysterious radio operator was, he was somewhere on a fifty mile line between the wireless truck and Barrow. Next time he broadcast, they'd be ready for him. No matter how fast he was.

Gallagher packed quickly. The important thing now was to put distance between himself and his transmission site. He knew that the RACS' monitoring was good; speed and mobility were his only allies. He had just jerked the antenna wire down from the oak when the genuine fishing line he had cast into the stream suddenly started paying out with a loud scream from the reel. The unattended rod started slivering through the autumn leaves toward the stream.

With a loud yell of 'Be Jesus!' Gallagher dropped everything and dived for the disappearing rod.

The cipher clerk ripped the message off the roll and handed it to Kneller.

'He's in the Barrow area,' the aide said, 'and will start looking for the U-boat tomorrow.'

Doenitz held his hand out for the signal.

'Why has he signed himself "St Peter"?'

Kneller grinned. 'He's posing as a fisherman. Berlin did warn us that he's got a sense of humour.'

*　　*　　*

Gallagher wasn't usually keen on fresh-water fish, but the four-pound pike he had fried on his Primus had been delicious and was ample compensation for the inconvenience of having to pitch his tent in near darkness.

A cold wind was blowing across the desolate fells as he prepared for a well-earned night's sleep. He drained his mug of whiskey-laced cocoa and contemplated the evil-looking pike's head that he had jammed like a mascot under the motorcycle's headlamp. He patted it affectionately before crawling into his sleeping bag.

'May you bring me luck tomorrow, Fergus, me boy.'

48

Leymann had been right when he had guessed that Stein would make trouble. By lunchtime the following day every prisoner of war in Grizedale Hall had heard the sub-lieutenant's bleak version of *U700*'s surrender and the part played by Anders.

Anders was miserably aware of the changed atmosphere as he lined up for his meal. The clatter of cutlery on enamel plates was subdued, and there wasn't the usual clamour of mealtime conversation. He sensed that what little discussion there was concerned him and *U700*.

He picked a knife and fork out of the chipped basins and made his way to the table at the back of the hall, keeping to the wall so that he wouldn't have to walk between the rows of trestle tables. He was aware of 200 pairs of eyes following him – in particular Kretschmer's and Stein's and the two giant, ex-*Bismarck* gunnery officers who Stein hadn't wasted time in befriending.

Shulke was alone; the other officers who normally used

the table were sitting elsewhere. Anders sat opposite him and got straight on with the business of eating – bony elbows tucked in, head down, and looking neither to the left nor right. Shulke guessed that it would be better for the time being to say nothing.

There was a movement at the other end of the room. Shulke looked up and was alarmed to see that Stein, Schumann, and Kirk were carrying their trays toward their table. Without a word the three sat down: Stein dropped into the seat beside Shulke, and Kirk and Schumann – grinning broadly – sat on either side of Anders.

Stein began to tear pieces of bread off his regulation midday slice, chewing deliberately while keeping his eyes fixed on Anders.

'What do you want, Stein?' Shulke demanded.

Stein smiled and brushed imaginary crumbs from his spotless jacket before speaking. 'There's something that we'd like to learn from you, major.'

'Learn what?' Shulke was in no mood for guessing games.

'Something that will be very useful to all of us if we're stuck in this place for any length of time.'

'Learn what?' Shulke repeated irritably.

'How to eat with a coward.'

Shulke stiffened.

'You make it look so easy,' Stein continued, delicately placing another piece of bread between his gleaming teeth. 'Or is it a case of birds of a feather?'

Shulke started to grab Stein, but Anders quickly reached out a restraining hand. 'Don't, Conrad. It's what he wants.'

'Push off, Stein,' Shulke growled. 'And take your little friends with you.'

Stein continued to smile. 'Anders knows what I want. Shall I tell you?'

145

'The same sort of thing that your parents deserve for having you,' Shulke snapped.

Kirk's huge hand whipped across the table and seized Shulke by the collar. 'Do you know what a bosun's sabre is, major?' he asked, his voice a menacing rumble.

'I'm not in the slightest bit interested in naval affairs,' Shulke replied, disengaging his shirt from Kirk's powerful fingers.

Kirk thrust a massive thumb under Shulke's nose. '*That's* a bosun's sabre, major. Like to see what it can do?'

Kirk's left thumbnail was at least half an inch too long. The surplus nail had been carefully filed and honed to a razor edge along half its width. The other half consisted of serrations that appeared capable of slitting a man's jugular vein. It looked a deadly weapon when used by an expert, and Shulke had no doubt that Kirk was an expert.

There was a sudden rapping noise. Faulk was standing and banging for silence with a spoon. 'Gentlemen, Lieutenant-Commander Kretschmer has a statement to make.'

There was an immediate silence as Kretschmer rose, a silence that only the man who had caused more destruction than any other naval commander in world history could command.

'Lieutenant Bernard Anders,' said Kretschmer tonelessly. 'Will you stand up please.'

Anders stood like a man in a trance.

'As you all know,' said Kretschmer, 'Anders is here because his U-boat was bombed by the RAF, and as you also know, we treated British claims that *U700* surrendered without a fight as enemy propaganda. We now know that those reports are true.'

Kretschmer paused. He knew he didn't have to continue – he could merely deliver a speech that roundly castigated Anders. Then he noticed that Stein and the two *Bismarck* gunners were sitting at Anders' table, and he realized he had no choice.

'It has been decided that from now on, no officer will speak to, communicate, or attempt to communicate with Lieutenant Anders in any way whatsoever.' Kretschmer managed to catch Stein's eye. 'A serious view will be taken if anyone disobeys this order. I'm going to speak to Anders now, and I want it clearly understood that I shall be the last person to do so until further notice.' He paused. 'Lieutenant Anders, do you have anything to say?'

Unable to reply, Anders shook his head slowly.

'The British have an expression for your punishment, lieutenant,' Kretschmer said. 'It is called being sent to Coventry.'

Kretschmer sat. The whole wretched business had left a bad taste in his mouth, but he hoped to God the scheme worked.

Anders subsided into his chair. Shulke was too shocked for the full implication of Kretschmer's words to sink in. He opened his mouth to speak to Anders, but heard Stein say, 'One word to him, major. Just one word . . .'

Stein's smile was pleasant, but his voice was menacing.

Part Three

49

'Ten bob,' the boatman said sourly.

Gallagher looked askance at the rowboat. There were two inches of water in the bottom, and the thwarts were splattered with gull droppings. 'I said I wanted to hire it – not buy it,' he said.

The boatman spat over the harbour wall into the sea. 'Ten bob, and it's yours for the day.'

'You reckon it'll stay afloat for a day?'

The blast from a scruffy coaster heading toward the Meccano tangle of Barrow's dockland cranes drowned the boatman's reply. They eventually agreed on eight shillings for the day, and the boatman grudgingly helped load Gallagher's fishing tackle into the boat's stern sheets.

'Don't go beyond the *Falkus*,' the boatman warned as Gallagher cast off. 'Harbour master can get funny about people getting too near the submarine yard.'

By eleven o'clock the sun was pleasantly warm, and Gallagher had leisurely rowed nearly a mile along the broad reach toward Walney Island and the Vickers yard. The *Falkus* turned out to be an elderly rusting tramp that had hit a mine at the beginning of the war and was now kept afloat by its cargo of rotting pulp and old books.

Gallagher rowed languidly past the forlorn little coaster, up the narrowing estuary with its mud flats and screaming sea birds, which eventually gave way to the cranes and wharves of the ship and submarine construction yards. He had assembled a fishing rod and was trailing a line and float behind him in the water. He lay back against a rucksack, hands behind his head and cap pulled down over his eyes. Several pairs of binoculars had been trained on him at various times by various officials, and it had been decided that the dozing fisherman wasn't worth wasting patrol boat fuel to chase away.

But Gallagher wasn't dozing. He was wide awake and carefully examining every yard of the wharves, slipways and jetties that drifted by under the peak of his cap. There was such a confused mass of grey and camouflaged ships that Gallagher had some difficulty at first in discerning where one ship ended and another began. Eventually his brain created order out of the chaos, and he was able to detect the occasional low profile of a submarine. There were five 'S' class boats and even an old Holland. Then another on a slipway of a class that he didn't recognize, but it definitely wasn't a U-boat. After ten minutes he began to despair of ever finding *U700*. If it wasn't moored on the outside of the ships lining the basin where it could be hit by a torpedo, then he would have to tell Lorient that there was no point in the operation going ahead. It was puzzling; one thing that Gallagher had been taught about submarines was that they had delicate pressure hulls and that they were rarely moored between other ships. If *U700* was at Barrow, it ought to be visible from the water.

Gallagher was about to reel in his fishing line when he noticed a grey Bentley coupé driving along the quayside. He was certain that it was the same car that had nearly hit him the day before.

Brice was out of the car as soon as Fleming had applied the handbrake. He looked quickly around the wharf and was disappointed not to see the U-boat. Fleming showed their passes to a dockyard policeman who explained that they were welcome to go aboard and that the lights in the boat had been switched on.

Fleming gave the man a charming smile. 'Only one snag, old boy. Where exactly is the U-boat?'

The policeman pointed to a humped, tarpaulin-shrouded shape moored against the wharf. Brice had assumed from its small size that it was a refuelling pinnace. It was less than seventy yards long.

'That's it?' Fleming inquired incredulously.

'Nothing to 'em, is there, sir?' the policeman said. 'Was a shock for us all when it turned up. I'll give you a hand with the covers.'

It took less than five minutes for the policeman to unfasten the ropes and pull sufficient tarpaulin away from the central hump for Brice and Fleming to climb on to the bridge. The first thing Brice's engineer's eye noticed was the surplus metal that the welders had left when they had fixed the anti-spray lip around the outside rim of the conning tower. It was sound enough welding, but it hadn't been cleaned up: a sure sign of mass production and a shipyard working under pressure.

Fleming was first down the hatch. By the time Brice had climbed down into the control room, Fleming had the attack periscope out of the well and was eagerly peering through the eyepieces.

'Amazing,' he muttered. 'Absolutely amazing. Clear as a bell. Take a look at that.'

Brice looked through the eyepieces. Fleming had the periscope trained on an unsuspecting office girl who was sitting in the sun on a flight of steps eating sandwiches. Her skirt was hitched up around her thighs. It was an astonishingly clear picture.

'Zeiss optics,' Brice commented, 'the best.' There was

153

something fascinating about looking through a periscope, especially one that gave such a bright, clear image as this one. It turned easily too. Brice estimated that the lone fisherman sitting in the rowboat was at least half a mile away, and yet it was possible to see that man seemed to be sketching something on the flyleaf of a book.

Brice straightened up and looked curiously around the control room interior. There was nothing revolutionary about the design but the layout was good: all pipes and cables had been carefully routed so that they would be accessible in an emergency. The various depth and pressure gauges were large and sensibly located high so that they could be seen from any position in the control room and not be hidden by the operators when they were perched on their stools. The really amazing thing was the size of the U-boat's interior. It was incredibly small. Brice correctly guessed that dissent among the crew would invariably lead to trouble. And trouble in a submarine was as deadly as a depth charge exploding against the pressure hull.

'No wonder the devils are finding it easy to sink our ships if they show up on a periscope as clearly as this,' Fleming remarked, peering through the eyepieces again. He studied the lone angler and wondered if the fishing was worthwhile.

Brice examined the seals around the watertight door. 'What are you going to call it?'

Fleming didn't speak for a moment; he had swung the periscope head back to the girl. 'They're going to name it after the code name of the operation to bring it to Barrow. Graph, HMS *Graph*.'

Brice was examining a depth gauge. 'Hey, these things are calibrated to over two hundred metres – that's way over six hundred feet. Twice the depth our subs can dive to. And yours.'

Fleming shrugged. 'My Bentley can't do anything like the top speed marked on her speedo.'

'You don't design subs like cars,' Brice said. He paused and looked around the control room again. 'You know, I still can't believe I'm aboard a German U-boat.'

Fleming stepped through the watertight door. 'Come and have a look at the torpedo, old boy. See if you believe that.'

Brice carefully removed the inspection cover from the torpedo warhead and shined his torch inside. Fleming was stretched out on one of the drop-down bunks that lined each side of the U-boat's forward torpedo room, watching Brice anxiously.

'Sure it won't go off, old boy? Just the appearance of those things makes me nervous. I've never seen anything that was so obviously intended to go bang.'

Brice shook his head. 'It's not like a mine. There's no point in booby-trapping something that isn't likely to fall into enemy hands.' He fished a camera out of his bag and attached a flash gun.

'You scientists puzzle me,' Fleming said. 'You're not a bit like the chaps writers make you out to be. You have absolutely no scruples about pinching other peoples' ideas.'

Brice checked the camera's focus. 'I didn't invent the camera, but that doesn't prevent me using it,' he said. 'Why sweat to design something if it's already been done? You can then concentrate on trying to improve it.'

'Point taken,' Fleming agreed.

'My job,' the American continued, 'is to see that the US Navy has the best torpedo there is.'

'Do you know yet if that thing will help?'

'Ask me in a couple of weeks.'

Fleming hooked his hands together behind his head.

'You're a man of simple ambitions, old boy. Mine is even simpler – to make money.'

'You've done all right with me on that score,' Brice commented sourly.

Fleming chuckled. 'Not gambling, that's for fools. There are other ways though. And much more agreeable places to do them.'

'Such as?' Brice asked, aiming his camera at the warhead.

Fleming closed his eyes. 'For some reason the island of Jamaica always comes to mind.'

Brice fired the flash gun and then turned his attention to a spare warhead without a torpedo body that was resting on a wooden cradle. He tapped it with his foot. 'This spare is a conventional warhead fired by contact when the nose strikes the side of a ship. Seems you were right about the German's shortage of magnetic warheads.'

Fleming smiled. 'Maybe we'll soon be sending them a few of ours.'

Later that afternoon, by a stream on the high fells near Barrow, Gallagher carefully tore the flyleaf from his book on the Lake District and gently heated it over the Primus stove to activate the invisible ink. At the top of the page was the rough, freehand sketch he had made of the suspect submarine at Barrow. The centre of the page was blank.

Gallagher moved the paper in a circular motion above the flame watching the centre of the page intently. Soon, faint lines began to appear. The lines hardened, followed by a gradual emergence of fine detail to complete the picture: an accurate line drawing of a Type VIIC U-boat. Every detail matched the details in Gallagher's sketch. The submarine moored at Barrow was, beyond all doubt, a U-boat.

And the only U-boat at Barrow was *U700*.

He allowed the page to drop on the stove's hissing burner and grinned at the leering pike's head, still wedged under the motorcycle's headlight.

'Well, Fergus, my boy. Looks like you've brought me luck after all.' He patted the pike's head affectionately and looked up at the soaring elm for a suitable overhanging branch.

50

As had become usual, the swell of conversation was effectively silenced by Anders' appearance in the hall.

Not a head turned as he walked to the serving table and joined the line. Also, as usual, the line melted as those waiting for their lunch moved to vacant seats at the tables.

Anders collected his tray and cutlery and looked for somewhere to sit. There were plenty of spaces but nowhere where he could sit alone. He nervously approached a table occupied by six Luftwaffe officers at the back of the room where there were three vacant places on one of the long benches. As one, the six officers rose and silently dispersed themselves to various free places throughout the hall.

Anders sat at the empty table and began to eat.

At the head table, Kretschmer was angry at the way his instructions were being interpreted. Not talking to Anders did not mean treating him like a leper. He wondered how he could reword his order and then decided it wasn't possible.

'At least it's better than what might happen to him otherwise,' Leymann pointed out as if he had read Kretschmer's thoughts.

The one man in the hall who was bitterly ashamed of

what had been going on for the last six days was Conrad Shulke. He finally decided that to eat at the same table as Anders could not be construed as a disregard of Kretschmer's orders. He picked up his meal and crossed to Anders' table. With a defiant glance at Stein who was watching with unbridled hatred, he sat opposite Anders and proceeded to finish his meal.

'You've upset someone, major,' said Stein, watching Shulke lifting potatoes.

Shulke paused in his work. 'Who and why?'

Stein nodded to Kirk who was standing nearby. The giant gunnery officer gave Shulke a sickly smile. 'Kirk seems to think you're disobeying the commander's orders,' Stein observed, brushing an invisible speck from his wrist sling.

Shulke looked at the huge gunner with contempt and wondered how it was that such an obvious thug could become an officer. Kirk's hands looked capable of tying knots in lamp-posts.

'If your little friend thinks that,' said Shulke, resuming work, 'then I can only assume he is as stupid as he looks.'

Kirk stepped forward and carefully selected the largest of the potatoes that Shulke had dug up. He held the potato out at arm's length in fingers that resembled a bunch of bananas and began to squeeze. Shulke watched, fascinated; Kirk's knuckles went white. There was a cracking sound and water began to ooze between the straining fingers. Kirk slowly opened his hand exposing a mass of pulp that had once been a potato.

'Eat with Anders again,' Stein warned, 'and next time it won't be a potato.'

The little major watched the two men walk away and forced himself to face the unpleasant fact that he was scared.

*　　*　　*

Lillian Baxter was about to close the sickbay window when she noticed Anders. It was usual for two prisoners to work one plot, but Anders was working by himself planting winter cabbage seedlings. She realized she hadn't seen anyone working with him for several days.

As she watched, Kirk and Stein appeared from the far end of the plots and walked down one of the dividing paths. Kirk was pushing a wheelbarrow. The two men were laughing at a shared joke. Anders looked up at their approach. To Lillian's surprise, Kirk and Stein left the path and walked straight across Anders' careful handiwork. Not only that, they seemed to deliberately kick and trample on the freshly planted seedlings. What happened next was a series of events of an ugliness that was in no way diminished by its brevity: Anders grabbed a garden fork and lunged at Stein. Kirk knocked the fork to one side and swung a heavy blow at Anders that missed. Anders grabbed a handful of earth and flung it in Kirk's face. The giant gunner gave an enraged bellow and drove his fist into Anders' stomach. Other prisoners stopped work to watch but made no attempt to intervene. Anders' legs buckled under him. Stein hooked his right arm around Anders' throat from behind and hauled him to his feet. Shulke suddenly appeared with a rake, and he brought the back of it down on Kirk's shoulder just as the gunnery officer was aiming another blow at Anders' face.

By the time Lillian had reached the scene clutching her first aid box, six guards led by Sergeant Rogers had waded into the skirmish and had broken it up. Lillian saw another company of guards, rifles at the ready, fanning out along the wire fence that bordered the lake. The prisoners involved in the fight had melted away leaving Anders lying in the middle of his devastated vegetable plot.

'What was it all about?' Lillian asked Sergeant Rogers.

'A diversion,' the NCO replied. He pointed at the

soldiers checking the fence. 'That's why they're down there. Always look in the opposite direction when you see a diversion.'

'It didn't look like a diversion to me.'

'They're not supposed to.'

Lillian moved toward Anders. 'I'd better see if this one is okay.'

'Wouldn't bother,' Rogers said as he walked away. 'That's the one who's the troublemaker.'

Anders had climbed to his feet and was bending down to retrieve the few undamaged seedlings. Lillian stooped down and passed him a plant that had only one leaf broken off.

'I think this one might be all right.'

Anders took it and said nothing.

'*Was* it a diversion?' Lillian asked.

Anders did not look at her. 'Of course.'

Lillian realized it was useless.

'I've got the new brake bits for my car,' she said changing the subject. 'Major Veitch says it's okay for you to fit them if Lieutenant-Commander Kretschmer has no objections.'

Anders stared down at a seedling with torn roots.

Lillian stood up. 'Of course, you don't have to if you don't want to.'

Anders looked up at her. 'Yes,' he said uncertainly. Then he smiled. 'Yes, I would like to very much.'

51

At Lorient, a biting October wind was sweeping eastward across the desolate airfield, making mournful music in the untuned telegraph wires that skirted the perimeter fence near the hangers.

Doenitz examined the crack in the Junkers' undercarriage with a magnifying glass. The fuel that had been pumped into the aircraft was now draining back through the hoses into the storage tank.

'It's closing.'

Kneller and Goder stooped down to peer more closely at the crack that gradually became fainter as the Junkers shed the huge load that had been poured into its tanks.

Doenitz straightened up and thrust his hands into his greatcoat pockets. He stared at the cluster of iron bars that Goder had suspended between the Junkers' wheels to simulate the weight of a torpedo. 'Lucky you heard it crack before you started the taxi test.'

Goder nodded. He preferred not to think about what might have happened if the Junkers' undercarriage had collapsed with full tanks.

'Do you have a spare strut in stores?' Doenitz asked.

'Yes, admiral,' the pilot replied disconsolately. 'Fitting a new one is no problem. But there's nothing to stop it happening again.'

'Let's find someplace warm and discuss it over coffee,' Doenitz suggested.

Goder gratefully wrapped his numb fingers around the steaming mug and politely waited for Doenitz to speak first. Both Kneller and the admiral were studying the plans of the Junkers' drastically altered fuel system. It was some moments before Doenitz spoke.

'How much more fuel was to have been pumped aboard when you heard the crack?'

Goder put down his drink and pulled a clipboard toward him. 'Three hundred litres, admiral.'

Doenitz thoughtfully rubbed his chin. 'So presumably, cutting down your fuel load by six hundred litres would create a safety factor to prevent the Junkers being over-loaded?'

Goder smiled wanly. 'Please don't think I'm being facetious, admiral, but it's crazy to talk about safety factors and that Iron Annie in the same breath.'

'You haven't answered my question,' said Doenitz acidly.

Goder thought for a moment. 'Cutting down our fuel load by six hundred litres will enable us to take off, and that's all. We need every drop of fuel we can carry to find that U-boat.'

'But you have its exact position now,' Kneller pointed out.

Goder jabbed his finger at a graph on the clipboard. 'I've worked out our fuel requirements to the nearest eggcupful. We'll need that six hundred litres for inflight course corrections.' There was a hint of annoyance in the pilot's voice. He opened a map and pointed to the route that had been drawn with a heavy pencil. It was a huge semicircle that swept north-west out into the Atlantic, skirted Ireland to the west before turning toward England north of Ulster to approach Barrow from the north-west. The thick black line on the map resembled a giant reversed question mark.

'It's the circular course, admiral. Two thousand kilometres. If we could take a straighter line . . .'

'No,' Doenitz said sharply. 'You'd be cut down by enemy fighters before you crossed the English coast. Flying around Ireland will enable you to stay clear of trouble.'

'But it's a difficult course, admiral,' said Goder. 'We'll be making constant corrections – we'll have to. Flying at night, no landmarks, and a good probability of early morning fog in the target area.'

Doenitz realized what a seemingly impossible task he was setting Goder; the young navy pilot had little night-flying experience and had certainly never flown a four-thousand-kilometre round trip. Moreover, he would have to fly a dangerously weakened and overloaded aircraft in the hope of accomplishing a mission it had never been designed for.

There was a long silence in the room. All three men looked down at the map.

'There is one thing,' Doenitz said. 'Suppose I could arrange for a radio signal to be transmitted from the vicinity of the U-boat at fifteen minute intervals for three hours before your estimated time of arrival.'

Kneller looked blank at first, but Goder was astonished by the suggestion.

'A homing beacon, admiral?'

'Would it make a difference?'

It was then that Kneller understood what Doenitz had in mind. He opened his mouth to speak but was silenced by a withering stare.

'Well,' Goder said slowly, wrestling with the implication of what the admiral had said, 'every fifteen minutes . . . three hours . . .' He sat back and chewed his thumbnail. 'Yes, admiral, it would make all the difference in the world. We could fly straight to the target area.'

'On a safe fuel load?'

'Yes. We could remove one of the extra tanks.'

'Thank you, Goder,' Doenitz said. 'Would you leave us for a few minutes please?'

Goder got up and left the room.

'Admiral,' Kneller began earnestly, 'you realize what . . .'

Doenitz cut in harshly, 'If Gallagher wasn't prepared to take risks, John, he wouldn't have taken on the job in the first place.'

'But not unnecessary risks, admiral,' Kneller protested. 'He can't alter his frequencies. Mobility is his only hope

163

of escaping detection. To ask him to transmit for three hours at regular intervals from the same area would be the equivalent of signing his death warrant.'

'I want that U-boat destroyed before the British discover how deep it can dive and redesign their depth charges! The safety of my U-boat crews comes before anything else!'

Kneller said nothing.

'Gallagher's signals will not have to be so powerful to reach an aircraft in his vicinity,' Doenitz continued in a reasoning tone. 'He won't need a high aerial. It shouldn't be beyond his ingenuity to transmit while on his motor-cycle.'

Kneller stared at the far wall and eventually nodded his head. 'He'll be sent his instructions this evening.'

Just before 4:00 P.M. on that same day, Gallagher rigged his transmitter-receiver by a stream on the high fells and sat on his folding stool with the headphone pressed to his ear. He hoped that this would be the last call. He was confident he had provided his employer with more than enough information. With luck, he would be able to spend the rest of the stay in England getting on with some serious fishing.

The pike's head grimaced fixedly at him as he waited.

At four o'clock precisely, Lorient started talking to him. Gallagher's hand went to the horn button, and he rattled out his call sign and an acknowledgement.

But Lorient kept talking: '555,' they said. Gallagher frowned. The three digit code meant 'long message to follow,' which also meant that he'd have to be ready with a pencil and paper. He began to feel uncomfortable; a long message could mean a long reply – long enough for the army's direction-finding trucks to get a fix on him. He found a pencil and paper and told Lorient he was ready. It took three minutes to broadcast the text of the signal. When Lorient started the repeat, Gallagher had virtually covered the entire paper with groups of numbers. He allowed them to continue while he substituted the numbers for letters extracted from his book on fishing sites. It was a simple but safe code that used the text of a book held by both parties. It was less dangerous than providing the agent with an incriminating one-time code pad.

Gallagher was on the third line when he began to realize what they were asking him to do. He stopped writing and stared down at the sheet of paper as an icy serpent of fear coiled around his spine. His hand began to shake as he completed taking down the message. The headphone fell silent. Gallagher's fingers went to the horn button and hesitated. He knew he hadn't made a mistake – the wording of the signal made deadly sense: '. . . remain in vicinity of U-boat . . . every fifteen minutes . . .'

The palms of his hands were sweating now. The headphone had fallen from his fingers and was lying on the grass, bleeping imperiously. He picked it up and placed it against his ear. Did he understand the message? Would he obey instructions? Please acknowledge. Please acknowledge.

Gallagher gazed with unseeing eyes at the dancing, sparkling stream for a long moment before he slowly reached for the horn button with fingers that continued to tremble.

The army direction-finding truck was twenty miles east of Gallagher. The captain replaced the radio-telephone handset and smiled broadly at Corporal Anderson.

'I have a co-ordinate for you, corporal: one-seven-zero on a northern reciprocal.'

Anderson opened an adjustable protractor, set the angle and tightened the knurled screw. He placed the instrument's base on the straight edge at the bottom of the chart and slid the protractor along until its angled side was touching the centre of the cross on the map that marked the position of the second direction-finding truck. He drew a line across the map using the angled edge of the protractor – a line that intersected an existing line.

The captain studied the intersection point and nodded with satisfaction. 'Search all farmhouses and cottages within a two mile radius of that point, corporal, and we might find a radio transmitter. What was the signal strength?'

'Seven, sir.'

The captain scratched his chin. 'That was Charlie One's reading too. Which means that our talkative little friend is using a high, undirectional aerial – up a chimney, I dare say. Shouldn't be too difficult to find.'

Corporal Anderson looked at the sheet of paper covered with numbers. 'What about this, sir?'

'I'll pass it on to Brigadier Scott, but I doubt if they'll be able to crack it. They'll be using a one-time code pad.' The captain smiled suddenly. 'We'll move Charlie One and ourselves closer to Barrow. Next time our friend starts squawking we ought to be able to pin him down to within ten yards.'

Gallagher stared at the pike's head. 'Fergus, me boy,' he said. 'You're looking at a dead man.'

His voice was filled with sorrow rather than fear.

52

Stein counted slowly. Seven seconds had passed before the blinding searchlight beam returned like a comet to fill Grizedale Hall's ground floor laundry room with light.

'Two seconds longer than an hour ago,' Schumann said. 'See? I told you those tommies get tired of twiddling their lights in proper sequence.'

Another blaze of light swamped the room and departed, leaving rainbows dancing on Stein's retinas like demented roman candles. 'They're crazy,' he muttered. 'Why don't the idiots use floodlighting?'

'They tried,' said Schumann with a chuckle. 'We kept stealing the cable. Nine seconds that time. What are we waiting for?'

Kirk rose silently from the floor where he had been sitting like a giant Buddha. He scooped up the roll of cloth. An object inside the roll rattled metallically. The huge gunnery officer flashed his teeth in the dark in a grin of eager anticipation.

The three men pulled black woollen hoods over their heads. Apart from eye slits, their faces were completely covered.

'Okay,' Stein said, carefully timing his release of the window catch. 'Let's go and fix the little coward once and for all.'

It was nine o'clock and dark when Anders finished relining the brake shoes on the offside rear wheel of Lillian's station wagon. He looked at his watch and decided that there wasn't time to start the tricky task of refitting the brake drum. He had to be back in the hall in thirty minutes. He wiped his hands and looked at his handiwork with pride.

Apart from mealtimes, which were still an agony, he liked being alone. It was a legacy of a brotherless and sisterless childhood. All his life his parents had spent long hours working in the family bakery and had little time to attend to the needs of the undemanding boy who seemed content with his life, provided he could spend it in the public library.

Anders had done extremely well at school but was handicapped by a lack of self-confidence. He regarded his academic successes only as an indication of low standards set by his schools rather than a mark of any real ability. As a result he set himself impossible targets and then suffered from the belief that others secretly ridiculed him when he failed to achieve them. It was fear of ridicule that always haunted him. He never joined in team games because he dreaded the possibility of letting his side down by doing something stupid. He played chess but only because he could memorize all the openings in solitude and familiarize himself with classic games before exposing himself to the risks of competition. He easily beat his first opponent – his headmaster – in fifteen moves and then quickly convinced himself that the teacher had deliberately let him win to spare his feelings. For Anders, victories were also crushing defeats.

His father had served in U-boats during the Great War and had fond recollections of the spirit of comradeship that had existed among their crews. With the onset of the war, he felt his sensitive son would be happier serving in the newly-formed U-boat arm rather than in the world of harsh disciplines and traditions that characterized service on the 'big ships'.

The letter ordering Anders to report to submarine training school at Kiel had come at a time when he was on the brink of establishing a close relationship with his father. But it came 14 years too late, and Anders' short periods of leave during his initial training were insufficient to sustain the delicate flower of trust and understanding that had flourished so briefly and so splendidly between them.

It was inevitable that the break with home, coming at such a crucial time, meant Anders would unconsciously turn to Weiner as a substitute for his father.

And now, alone, friendless and miserable, a prisoner in a strange land far from home, Anders lived with the agonizing knowledge that his carelessness, his stupid lapse of attention at *U700*'s sky periscope, had led to a betrayal of Weiner's trust. And after that, as if seeking to atone for his betrayal, he had taken a loaded Luger onto the bridge and had pointed it at Weiner. When Weiner turned and saw the gun, his eyes, revealing a strange expression of sorrow that time would never erase, mirrored Anders' innermost feelings about himself. He was a failure, a despicable coward and, worst of all, a Judas.

It was a few minutes past nine. Anders shivered as he dropped the wrenches into the toolbox. He dreaded the nights in the dormitory, having to be first into bed, curled into the foetal position with the blanket pulled over his head.

Kretschmer's orders had been obeyed to the letter; the only time anyone spoke to him was when the British NCO bawled out his name at morning and evening roll calls.

There was a faint sound from the loft, a sudden creaking of roof timber. The noise was repeated, louder this time. Anders crossed the floor to the steep flight of steps that led to the hay loft. A muffled thud was followed by a shuffling noise that didn't sound like the noise rats would make. Anders' pulse quickened.

'Is anyone there?'

Silence answered.

He was about to put his foot on the first step when there was a sudden swish of displaced air. The tip of a homemade sword hit the step level with his eyes with such force that it splintered through the timber.

Before Anders could react he was knocked to the ground by a huge shape. Nor could he cry out for a mighty hand, like a giant bat, clamped itself over his mouth. 'Make one sound,' rasped a harsh, guttural voice an inch from his ear, 'and I lay a vein open so that you bleed like a pig.' It was Kirk pressing his 'bosun's sabre' hard against the side of Bernard's neck. 'You understand?'

'Yes,' Anders managed to croak.

A powerful push sent him reeling backward against the station wagon's radiator. The three masked figures advanced slowly toward him. They were dressed entirely in black. The middle figure was shorter than the other two, and his left arm was in a wrist sling. He was holding two swords in his right hand. He tossed one of them onto the flagstones beside Anders.

'Pick it up.'

Anders shook his head. 'I'm not going to fight you, Stein.'

Stein moved forward and pressed the tip of his sword hard against Anders' temple. 'You're going to fight, Anders. Everything is in your favour.' Stein held up his sling. 'Just the sort of handicap that would appeal to a coward.'

Anders looked at Kirk and Schumann in contempt. The two gunners were standing on either side of the stable. They looked like two gorillas watching for an opportunity to tear him to shreds.

'You have seconds . . .' Anders managed to say.

Stein flicked his blade experimentally back and forth under Anders' chin. 'They won't interfere.'

'I'm not going to fight you,' Anders repeated defiantly. He put his hand on the flagstones to push himself up, and as he did so his fingers touched the sword's crude hilt.

It was a mistake – a challenge duel started the instant an opponent touched his sabre. Anders looked up and saw the steel tip of Stein's sword lunging toward his throat.

* * *

Lillian pursed her lips in the mirror propped against the medicine cabinet and decided that lipstick was too scarce for her to waste any more trying to get the twin arches of her Cupid's bow exactly right.

She looked at her watch. Ten minutes past nine. David, her fiancé, had promised to pick her up at quarter past to run her home to Barrow. It was a nuisance having the station wagon out of commission – it meant having to fight David off on weekdays as well as weekends. Oh well . . .

A last check to make sure her seams were straight – her last pair of civilian stockings – and then lock up. She could hear the faint strains of the choir rehearsing in the main hall. God, how the Germans could sing. Her high heels clomped hollowly on the scrubbed linoleum floor. It was dark outside. For a moment she wished that she had obeyed standing orders by asking for two guards to escort her to the main gate. But the prisoners had never been any trouble and had always treated her with respect. Sergeant Rogers had explained that German prisoners accepted a measure of discipline that no British soldier would tolerate where women were concerned.

Anders threw himself to one side and the tip of Stein's sword blazed a wake of sparks across the flagstones where he had been lying. He lashed out at Stein with his feet and, to his surprise, felt his shoes connect with Stein's shins.

Stein overbalanced and began to topple forward, suddenly realizing that the wrist sling was a greater handicap than he had anticipated. The point of his sword jammed in a cracked flagstone and the weapon, unable to support his weight, snapped off six inches from the end of the blade. His wounded arm collided with the station wagon's headlight. The pain that lanced his arm was so intense he thought he was going to faint. He recovered just fast

171

enough to parry Anders' inexpert thrust at his side. The speed of Anders' recovery surprised Stein. Before he was properly on his feet and correctly balanced, he had to ward off two more thrusts. The missing six inches of blade was worrying; combined with Anders' long reach, it gave him a deadly advantage.

Stein drove forward for an opening, but Anders twisted sideways and deflected Stein's truncated blade. It was a neat move – one that would have meant the end for Stein had Anders been an expert. Nonetheless, it frightened Stein badly.

He sprang backward, moving lightly on his toes and feinting quickly to confuse Anders while he decided what to do. He noticed that Anders wasn't holding the hilt properly and realized it would be easy to disarm him. He feinted again, deliberately leaving himself open. Anders saw the opportunity and drove forward. Stein sidestepped adroitly and brought the flat of his blade down on Anders' sword with all his strength.

The shockwave raced up Anders' arm like a thousand volts and his sword clattered to the flagstones. He tried to grab the weapon but Stein, laughing, kicked it toward the station wagon. As Anders dived after it he tripped and fell heavily against the driver's door.

Stein pulled his mask off and smiled at Anders with thin, bloodless lips. He tossed his broken sword to Kirk, and picked up Anders' sword from the floor.

'Well now, Anders,' he said easily, 'you fight well for a coward.' He gestured to Kirk and Schumann. 'Now is the time, I think.'

The two bear-like gunnery officers removed their hoods. Grinning broadly Kirk walked slowly toward Anders, cracking his knuckles and flexing his broomstick fingers.

Anders climbed to his feet and backed away from the approaching giant. He didn't see Schumann edge around

172

behind him until it was too late. Schumann seized his arms and pinioned them to his side.

'Over the hood,' Stein said curtly.

Kirk arched Anders backward until he was lying across the station wagon's hood with his back crushed against the radiator. Schumann hooked Anders' feet under the front bumper, his cry of pain stifled by Kirk's suffocating hand.

Stein stood over his victim and rested the tip of the sword on Anders' belt. 'Don't worry, Anders,' he said with a cold smile. 'I'm not going to kill you. But I am going to make sure you're the last of your cowardly line.'

With that he moved the sword's jagged tip downward.

Lillian was passing the stable when she heard a faint whimper. Frowning, she walked to the double doors. They were locked. She peered through a crack in the doors. It was some seconds before she could make out what was happening inside the stable and then she saw them: two men standing on either side of the car appeared to be holding something down on the hood. A third man had his back to her. He was holding a sword.

Suddenly Lillian was hammering on the double doors and screaming for help.

53

Major Veitch snatched the two swords up off his desk and held them angrily under Kretschmer's nose. The German officer did not flinch but kept his eyes fixed steadily on the British officer.

'What about these?' Veitch demanded. 'Have you felt their edge? Do you honestly expect me to believe . . .'

'Major Veitch,' Kretschmer interrupted calmly. 'This is an internal discipline problem, and I give you my solemn word that there is no Nazi bullying going on.'

Veitch tossed the swords contemptuously on his desk. 'One of those men could've been killed last night.'

'It was a duel. Nothing more.'

'A duel? Is that how civilized men behave in your country?'

Not a muscle moved in Kretschmer's face. He stared hard at the British major until Veitch was forced to drop his gaze. 'It's a tradition, major, in which, as we've seen, no one gets hurt.'

Veitch shook his head. 'Nurse Baxter is of the opinion that Anders would've been hurt if she hadn't raised the alarm.'

Kretschmer remained silent.

Veitch watched the German's face. 'Nurse Baxter is also of the opinion that Lieutenant Bernard Anders is being systematically bullied,' he stated flatly.

'If she has concrete evidence of that,' Kretschmer replied dispassionately, 'then I'd be most grateful if her evidence could be passed on to me so that I can deal with the culprits.'

It was the longest sentence that Veitch had ever heard from the aloof German officer. 'I sincerely hope you are able to stamp out this bullying without evidence from us,' Veitch said caustically. 'Because if you don't, the War Office most certainly will. I hope I make myself clear.' He stood. 'Good day, commander.'

Kretschmer returned Veitch's salute, turned on his heel and strode out of the office. Leymann was waiting outside. The tubby lawyer had to trot to keep up with Kretschmer as he walked angrily to the main hall.

'He's agreed to transfer Anders?' Leymann asked.

'No.'

Leymann was surprised. 'Why not?'

Kretschmer stopped to unwrap and light a cheroot. 'Because that's not what I asked for. I'm not going to unload the problem on another senior German officer at another camp.'

Leymann shrugged. 'So you let Anders stay. Stein or some other hothead will kill him, and it's no more than he deserves.'

'He deserves a fair trial,' Kretschmer said coldly.

'And what do we do in the meantime while we're waiting for the invasion of England?'

'You're to appoint bodyguards to keep a round-the-clock watch on Anders. Luftwaffe men would be best.'

'That won't cure the basic problem.'

Kretschmer blew out a thin cloud of smoke. 'I know, Willi. That's why we'll have to think of something that will solve the problem once and for all.'

54

Fleming parked his Bentley beside *U700*, trotted nimbly along the gangplank on the U-boat's deck casing, and disappeared down the hatch. Brice was too absorbed in his work to notice Fleming's arrival.

'Morning, Alan,' Fleming said breezily, hoisting himself on to a bunk. He pointed at a framed photograph hanging from a handwheel. 'Who's the charming lady? Your wife?'

Brice nodded and then yawned widely. 'I sent her a cable giving her my solemn word I'll be home in time for Thanksgiving.'

'You look all in,' Fleming commented sympathetically.

Brice smiled and reached for a Thermos bottle. 'The plant cafeteria has concocted a special brew for me to keep me awake. Like some?'

Fleming sniffed the flask's contents suspiciously. 'What does it taste of?'

'Acorns. They claim that it's coffee. It keeps me awake worrying what it's doing to me.'

'Thank you, no,' Fleming said. 'Actually, I'm going back to London, so unless you want a lift back, I've just dropped in to say cheerio.'

'Thanks, Ian, but I don't want to miss the test dive. A skeleton crew and two scientists are taking her out at daybreak next Tuesday.'

'How deep?'

'Two hundred feet to start with.'

Fleming's elegant features creased into a grimace. 'Rather you than me, old boy.'

Brice grinned. 'This baby's good for six hundred feet.'

'Bring it back in one piece,' Fleming said, jumping down from the bunk. 'There's a plan afoot to open it to the public for a few days. Oh well, I daresay our paths will cross in London.'

'They'd better,' Brice growled. 'I want to win some of my money back.'

Fleming laughed as he stepped through the watertight door. 'Not a chance.'

'Hold on, Ian,' Brice said, rummaging through the notes and diagrams that were strewn across the torpedo room floor. He straightened up and held out a paper bag. 'A small token of my appreciation. I'm very grateful for all you've done.'

Fleming accepted the bag, looked inside, and took out a book entitled *Birds of the West Indies*.

'You said you wanted to live in Jamaica after the war,'

Brice said quickly. 'I thought it might be useful. The girl in the shop said that James Bond was a world authority on birds.'

Fleming, touched by the gesture, shook Brice's hand warmly. 'That's jolly decent of you, Alan. Thanks very much indeed.' He paused and looked down at the partially dismantled torpedo. 'How's the scientific espionage progressing?'

'It's a fine torpedo,' Brice said. 'I've learned a helluva lot in the last few days.' He paused and then grinned broadly. 'Espionage, eh? Well, for all intents and purposes I guess I really am on His Majesty's Secret Service, aren't I?'

55

The mess hall had been converted for a Council of Honour, and the first thing Anders noticed when he walked in was the large, homemade Kreigsmarine flag, with its central black swastika, that was mounted on one wall.

'Council of Honour,' Shulke had scoffed the previous day. 'They're mounting a court-martial – an illegal court-martial at that.'

The double doors closed behind Anders, and the two Luftwaffe officers who had acted as his bodyguards since the incident in the workshop marched beside him through the rows of seated prisoners. Anders guessed that the entire camp was present.

Faulk was seated at a table directly beneath the flag. In front of him was a long table with Conrad Shulke sitting at one end and Willi Leymann at the other. The first row of chairs was occupied by Kretschmer – smartly turned out with the Knight's Cross gleaming at his throat – and Sub-Lieutenant Richard Stein.

Anders took his place beside Shulke. Faulk stood – the signal for everyone present to rise to their feet.

'Lieutenant Bernard Anders, Mr President,' one of the Luftwaffe officers announced.

'Thank you,' Faulk said.

The two Luftwaffe officers clicked their heels in unison, saluted, and marched back to the doors. They would remain within earshot of the alarm system that would alert them if and when the British approached.

Anders caught Shulke's eye. The whole business was turning out to be a more elaborate farce than either of them had anticipated.

'You will remain standing, Lieutenant Anders,' said Faulk, as he sat down, motioning everyone else to do likewise. 'There are two charges against you. One: as acting commander of a U-boat, you displayed cowardice in the face of the enemy. Two: that you failed to obey battle orders by scuttling your U-boat to prevent it from falling into enemy hands. How do you plead to these charges?'

Anders followed Shulke's instructions by remaining silent.

'How do you plead to these charges!' Faulk repeated.

Conrad Shulke stood. 'I've been studying the Geneva Convention, gentlemen. It's an interesting document. Not only does it lay down standards for the treatment of prisoners-of-war by their captors, but it also lists the responsibilities of the prisoners. The holding of courts-martial by prisoners is expressly forbidden.'

'If you are addressing me,' Faulk said, 'you will address me as Mr President. Otherwise I will nominate someone else to conduct Lieutenant Anders' defence.'

'Germany is a signatory of the Geneva Convention,' Shulke said tartly.

Leymann rose. Prison diet was improving his figure but not the fit of his uniform. 'Mr President, I have explained to Major Shulke that this is a Council of Honour and not a court-martial. It will hear the evidence that is available and *recommend* a sentence – not pass one. Afterward, Lieutenant Anders will be able to join in all normal camp activities and mention of, or reaction to in any form, the *U700* affair will be forbidden until we are liberated after the invasion.'

'If I'm to defend Lieutenant Anders,' Shulke said, 'it is my duty to challenge the legality of this council.'

Faulk nodded. 'Fine – you've challenged it. Now let's get on. How does your defendant plead to the charges?'

'Not guilty,' Shulke muttered and sat down.

Leymann hauled himself to his feet. The plump Bavarian lawyer was obviously enjoying himself. He read Anders' statement to the gathering and briefly outlined the circumstances that led to *U700*'s surrender. Then he turned to Faulk. 'For my first witness, Mr President, I wish to call Sub-Lieutenant Richard Stein.'

Stein stood very straight. He had gone to considerable pains over his appearance even by his standards; his blond hair had been carefully brushed and his shirt stiffened with starch obtained by boiling a potato. He answered Leymann's searching questions in a clear, resolute voice, without sparing Anders a single glance. The final questions dealt with the round robin – the document that Stein had circulated to the crew of *U700* before the armed trawlers and destroyer had arrived.

'Every member of the crew pledged their support for Lieutenant Anders if he were to arrest the captain and countermand the surrender?'

'Yes,' Stein replied. 'Everyone signed. There would have been no question of Anders having to cope with divided loyalty if he had arrested Weiner.'

Leymann lowered his bulk on to his chair. 'No more questions, Mr President.'

Shulke stood and referred to his notes. 'You said that the RAF do not possess an air-borne depth charge, Lieutenant Stein, but only an anti-submarine bomb that is useless unless it scores a direct hit. Correct?'

'Correct,' Stein said crisply.

Shulke smiled. 'Not all of us here are naval men so perhaps I had better enlarge. A bomb explodes on the surface of the water and has to hit a U-boat to be certain of harming it. A depth charge explodes beneath the surface and can cause severe damage to a U-boat even if it misses?'

'Correct,' Stein repeated. 'But the RAF do not have an air-borne depth charge.'

Shulke relaxed – Stein had walked into the trap. 'They most certainly do now. The three new arrivals this morning are survivors from a U-boat that was destroyed by depth charges dropped by a Sunderland flying boat. If necessary, I shall be calling them as witnesses.'

Stein remained silent, and Shulke began to feel more comfortable in his unfamiliar roll of inquisitor.

'Did you see this "bomb" fall?' he asked.

Stein hesitated momentarily. Then, 'No.'

'Why not?'

'I ducked. It's customary when a bomb falls – it helps you live longer.'

There was some laughter, which Faulk silenced with his homemade gavel.

Shulke remained outwardly unruffled. 'Did Captain Weiner duck?'

'I don't think so.'

'You don't think so,' Shulke's tone was scathing. 'So

you've no idea if the Hudson dropped a bomb or an infinitely more deadly pattern of depth charges. You ducked while Weiner bravely watched the Hudson all the time.'

'Bravely?' Stein echoed incredulously. 'He was paralysed with fear!'

'Did he wave his shirt after the Hudson dropped the depth charges?'

'Yes.'

'Immediately after? Before it had time to turn?'

'Yes. He tore it off in panic.'

Shulke frowned. 'But just now you said that Weiner was *paralysed* with fear! If Weiner was paralysed with fear and yet managed to get his jacket off, and tear off his shirt to wave at the Hudson, we can only conclude that you helped him!'

It was a wild guess yet it produced a reply that caused a murmur of surprise among the prisoners.

'I helped him off with his jacket and shirt because I thought he'd been injured by a bomb splinter.'

'Nevertheless, you helped Weiner and therefore played a significant part in *U700*'s surrender!'

Stein's face paled. 'That's a damned lie! I was the only one who fought that Hudson! Look!' He jerked back his sleeve revealing the bandage wrapped around his left forearm. 'This was caused by a round of 303 machine-gun fire from the Hudson's front turret.'

'Exactly, lieutenant!' Shulke barked. 'You were injured – you were carried unconscious to your berth, and you weren't in the control room after the attack. In view of this, how can you expect this council to believe you when you say, as you said in your evidence, that *U700* was undamaged after the attack and was capable of diving? And why, may I ask, should we take the word of a man who needs the support of a couple of thugs before creeping out of the hall at night to attack Lieutenant Anders as he worked alone in the stables!'

There was an outburst of jeering and catcalls directed at Shulke from the prisoners.

Leymann bobbed to his feet. 'Mr President, I feel that the council must instruct Major Shulke to stick to the issue and not resort to shouting abuse at the witness on irrelevant and unsubstantiated matters.'

'I have no more questions,' said Shulke, sitting down and folding his arms.

'In that case, I would like to call my next witness,' said Leymann. 'Lieutenant Bernard Anders please.'

Leymann looked smugly confident as Anders moved to the witness table and recited the oath. He carefully tidied his notes before addressing Anders.

'Were you paying close attention when Lieutenant Stein was giving his evidence?'

'Yes.'

'Excellent. Is there any part of his account that you wish to dispute or refute?'

'No,' Anders replied.

'Why didn't you relieve Weiner of command after the surrender?' Leymann asked, his tone mild. 'You knew that you had the support of the crew.'

'Because that would constitute a mutiny,' Anders replied resolutely.

'You went to training college?'

Anders sensed trouble. 'Yes.'

'Were you not taught the difference between mutiny and the justified relieving of command?'

'Yes.'

Leymann thrust his thumbs into his waistband and watched Anders carefully. 'Please tell the council the difference.'

'I can't remember the exact wording.'

'Then give us an inexact rendering.'

Anders thought for a moment. 'Mutiny is the refusal to obey the lawful commands of a senior officer. Justified relieving of command is . . .'

Leymann pounced the instant Anders faltered. 'Justified relieving of command is when the senior officer has demonstrated by his actions or inaction that he is no longer capable, either mentally or physically, of issuing lawful commands! Isn't that right?'

'Yes.'

'After the attack by the Hudson, you said in your statement that you went on to the bridge and found Weiner in a state of shock. A state of shock! Your own words! So why didn't you relieve him of command there and then?'

Anders stared at Leymann and wondered if he had the courage to blurt out the one thing that he had not mentioned in his statement: that at the crucial moment during the surfacing drill, he had taken his eyes away from the sky periscope.

But Leymann didn't wait for an answer. 'Didn't Lieutenant Stein *passionately* urge you to assume command?'

'I – I didn't trust him.'

'You didn't trust him,' Leymann repeated sarcastically. 'And yet every member of the crew signed that pledge. What was the matter, Anders? Wasn't that enough for you? Did you want their signatures in blood?'

Shulke half-rose to object but Leymann was relentlessly hounding his prey – determined to drive Anders into an inescapable corner. 'And still you refused to act! Nor did you act after Weiner abandoned the boat and paddled to the destroyer. You were left in command then!'

Anders looked up at his tormentor. 'No. The captain of the British destroyer was technically in command of the U-boat after the surrender.'

183

'You worried about legal niceties when there was a danger of your boat falling into enemy hands?'

'I was worried for the safety of the crew.'

Leymann ignored the answer. 'Why didn't you give the order to abandon ship so that you could scuttle the boat? There was plenty of time.'

'How could I when the British had threatened to open fire if I allowed the crew on deck?' Anders demanded.

'Didn't it occur to you that they wanted to prevent you scuttling?'

'I thought they were worried in case we tried to man the main gun.'

'And you refused Lieutenant Stein's offer to jump into the water to see if they were bluffing?'

'I was worried for the safety of the entire crew including Lieutenant Stein. In the heat of the moment I felt as Commander Weiner did – that the lives of the crew were more important than the capture of the boat.'

Leymann adopted a puzzled tone. 'Surely you realized that the secrets revealed to the enemy could lead to the deaths of countless sailors in the future? That the entire U-boat offensive could be endangered?'

'I've told you what my thoughts were,' said Anders. 'And besides – everything of value in the boat was destroyed.'

'Except the magnetic torpedo in one of the bow tubes!' Leymann roared. 'The one thing that the enemy wanted above all else!' Leymann regarded his victim with contempt. 'So you thought of nothing else but your own skin and the skin of the crew?'

Anders failed to see the inherent danger in the double-edged question and blundered into the lawyer's trap. 'Yes,' he began. 'But . . .'

'*Yes!*' Leymann thundered triumphantly. '*Yes!*' He

looked at the assembly as if seeking confirmation of Anders' guilt.

'Do you realize what your reply means?' he asked softly.

Anders shrugged. 'What does it matter what I say? You'll only twist it to mean something else.'

'Do you wish to reconsider?'

'I just want all this over. All I can say is that at the time I saw no point in needless killing and I had no wish to die myself. I saw nothing wrong in that. Now I don't care very much if I do die.'

Leymann gathered up his notes. 'I have no more questions for this coward.'

Faulk looked inquiringly at Shulke. 'Major Shulke?'

Shulke rose slowly to his feet and considered his words. 'My own definition of coward,' he said quietly, 'is someone who has the courage to show that he's not a hero.'

There was a silence that was broken by Faulk. 'Very well. The Council of Honour will now retire to consider its verdict.'

Everyone in the hall rose. Faulk, Kretschmer, Stein, Leymann, and Shulke left the hall by a side door. Shulke turned and gave Anders a brief smile as he turned to close the door behind him.

Anders sensed that another ordeal was about to begin. Before him was a sea of silent, expressionless faces. No one spoke. No one stirred. There was no overt movement or gesture from any individual that might set them apart from the other members of the mob. For that's exactly what they were. A mob. A controlled mob. A point-us-in-any-direction-and-we'll-fix-them mob.

Then someone started to hiss. It was, as is usual with mob behaviour, the signal for others to join in. The hissing spread, a venomous expression of hatred for something that they didn't understand and didn't want to understand.

A wad of newspaper smacked against Anders' cheek.

Another struck him on the forehead. Two more missed. A fifth hit his eye and produced tears.

The hissing stopped abruptly as the door opened and the members of the council filed back and took their places. They had been out of the room for less than three minutes. The prisoners waited for Faulk to sit, but he remained on his feet, grim-faced and silent.

Then he cleared his throat. 'Lieutenant Bernard Anders,' he said, 'you have been found guilty of failing to scuttle your ship to prevent it from falling into enemy hands. You have also been found guilty of displaying cowardice in the face of the enemy.' Faulk paused and referred to a piece of paper. 'With one dissension, the recommended sentence of the Council of Honour is that you be hanged at a convenient time and place as soon as this war is over.'

56

The next morning Lillian pushed the stable doors open and found Anders working on the last wheel of her station wagon.

'Good morning, Bernard,' she said cheerfully, kneeling beside him. 'How's it going?'

'Okay,' Anders replied without looking at her.

'I'm supposed to be meeting my fiancé tomorrow evening. I was wondering if you'll be finished in time.'

'It'll be ready tomorrow.'

Lillian smiled. 'You said that yesterday.'

'There was a holdup in the afternoon.'

Lillian became serious. 'I'm seeing Major Veitch later this morning to thank him for allowing you to repair the car. Is there anything you'd like me to mention to him for you?'

Anders fitted a wrench to the brake's cable adjustor. 'Such as?'

'Such as a transfer to another camp.'

'I'm okay here.'

Lillian frowned. 'I'm not blind, Bernard.'

'It was a duel. Friendly sword play. An old tradition.'

'I don't mean that,' said Lillian sharply. 'I'm talking about *U700*.'

Anders nearly dropped the wrench.

'The papers didn't give names of the crew,' she said, 'but it was your boat, wasn't it?'

'What if it was?'

'It surrendered. It was in all the papers. It doesn't need much intuition to guess that Kretschmer wouldn't look kindly upon someone involved in the surrender of a U-boat.'

Anders shrugged. 'Not if the surrender was unavoidable.'

Lillian began to get angry. 'Don't treat me as being completely stupid, Bernard. David, my fiancé, works at Barrow at Vickers. In two weeks time they'll be opening *U700* to the public. He said there was so little damage done to it that he couldn't understand why it surrendered.'

Anders spun the brake drum. 'I wasn't the captain. The surrender has nothing to do with me.'.

Lillian looked at him for a few moments and then sighed. 'I can't blame you if you don't want to talk. I am the enemy, I suppose.' She got to her feet and moved to the doors. 'But if you do need help, Bernard, please don't be afraid to ask.'

Anders stared at the brake drum after Lillian had left, thinking about what she had said. He remembered hearing a guard mention that he had a girl friend in Barrow. That meant that the town, or whatever it was, could not be far away.

The map of northern England was still in the station wagon's glove compartment. No doubt Major Veitch would burst a blood vessel if he knew about Lillian's carelessness. Anders spread it out on the floor and found Barrow almost immediately.

Amazingly, it was less than twenty miles from Grizedale Hall.

'Barrow?' Leymann echoed, his round, moon-like face sagging in amazement. 'Is he sure?'

Kretschmer nodded. 'It makes sense, Willi – a large submarine works with the expertise to assess the U-boat's capabilities. We should have guessed the British would send it there.'

Leymann looked down at the map. 'About twenty miles. What's that? Thirty kilometres?'

Kretschmer leaned back in his chair and lit a cheroot. 'A five hour walk across country for him, Willi.'

'You would send *him?*'

Kretschmer exhaled a cloud of smoke. 'It's his idea, Willi.'

'It's his fault the damned boat's there in the first place,' Leymann growled.

'That's why he ought to be given the chance to destroy it.'

'He wouldn't last five minutes out there,' Leymann protested. 'His English is barely passable.'

'Shulke has agreed to help him with it.'

Leymann stared at his senior officer. 'You really think Anders could do it?'

Kretschmer gave a ghost of a smile. 'If he survives the escape method that he's suggested. But he'll need a bomb – a substantial bomb – to blow that U-boat in half.'

57

Stein started counting as soon as the searchlight beam burst into the laundry room. He signalled to Anders and Kirk. The gunnery officer pushed his tools into his pockets and scooped up the roll of stair carpeting.

'Now!' Stein whispered as he pushed the window open.

Anders and Kirk dropped to the ground and dived for cover behind a group of shrubs. Kirk tightened his grip on the roll of narrow carpeting as a beam swept over their heads. Then the giant gunner was running, chasing the beam, with Anders close on his heels. They threw themselves flat as the beam completed its traverse of Grizedale Hall's facade and swung back in the opposite direction, passing above the two men. Kirk jabbed Anders in the ribs and ran toward the administration compound following an erratic route that utilized cover provided by the scattered trees. Anders, following close behind, was amazed at the gunner's ability to move like a cat despite his size.

They reached the high barbed-wire fence that surrounded the camp armoury. Kirk produced two pairs of stiff leather gloves. He and Anders stood on one end of the carpet roll and heaved it high into the air so that it dropped neatly over the fence near one of the concrete posts. When they went over the fence, using the carpet as protection against the needle-sharp barbs, their weight wouldn't leave a telltale sag in the wire. They pulled on their gloves and moments later were over the fence without difficulty. They disentangled the carpet and hid it under the autumn leaves for the return journey. Leaving it in place had been considered too risky.

The camp armoury was a substantial concrete hut protected by a heavy steel door and a massive padlock. Kirk examined the padlock by the light of a candle that Anders held cupped in his hands. Then he started to probe the interior of the lock with a variety of small tools and pieces of stout wire. The candle was beginning to burn Anders' hands.

'Come on,' he muttered impatiently.

Three minutes passed before Kirk grunted in satisfaction. There was a faint metallic click and the padlock fell open.

Anders followed Kirk into the armoury and pulled the door shut. He held the candle high and sucked in his breath in amazement. They were in an Aladdin's Cave of rifles, anti-riot equipment, small arms and ammunition. Kirk chuckled and held a hand grenade under Anders' astonished nose.

'No throwing stick,' said the giant gunner, grinning broadly. 'But I guess they still make a nice bang, eh? How many do you want?'

The events and planning of the past twenty-four hours had restored Anders' self-respect, giving him a degree of self-confidence he had never known before.

He set the box down on Kretschmer's desk and was able to meet the cold, watching eyes.

'You have everything?' Kretschmer demanded.

'Everything,' Anders said, reaching into the box and placing the items on Kretschmer's desk. 'Two kilos of wet clay, an alarm clock, a shoebox, string – and these.' Anders set six hand grenades in a neat row on the desktop, and Kretschmer picked one up and examined it curiously.

It was quite unlike the German grenade. Instead of a hollow throwing handle that contained the friction ignitor, there was a pin that passed through two diecast ears

190

below the neck of the grenade. The pin held a curved, spring-loaded lever against the grenade's body.

'Pull that pin out,' Anders said, 'and the lever flies up and starts an eight-second fuse. They're not as good as ours because you can't carry several in your boots, but they're ideal for making a bomb.'

Kretschmer pushed the six hand grenades across to Anders. 'Show me,' he invited.

Anders pressed several handfuls of soft clay into the shoebox and picked up one of the grenades. He held the lever firmly and withdrew the pin. Still holding the lever in place, he gently pushed the grenade lever side down into the bed of clay in the shoebox and then packed more clay tightly around the grenade's body.

Anders smiled. 'This is the awkward part.'

Slowly, Anders removed his hand from the grenade. The clay held the lever safely in place. Anders dropped the pin on the desk.

Five minutes later there were five pins on Kretschmer's desk and five grenades packed into clay in the shoebox.

A large space at one end of the box comfortably accepted the alarm clock. The bells had been removed and a length of string had been tied to the key that wound the alarm. Anders tied the other end of the string to the pin on the sixth grenade and fitted it into the shoebox. The sixth grenade was the only one with its pin still in place.

'That's it,' Anders said, wiping the clay from his fingers. 'The alarm goes off, winds the string around the key as it turns and pulls the pin out of the priming grenade. It explodes, shatters the clay around the other five grenades, which all explode together eight seconds later.'

'Neat,' Kretschmer said. 'Are you sure the clock key develops enough power to pull the pin out of the grenade?'

'Plenty,' Anders said.

Kretschmer opened a drawer and placed a .38 Webley

revolver on the desk. 'Kirk took it from the armoury.' He slid it across to Anders. 'You'll need it to get aboard the U-boat.'

Anders shook his head. 'I don't think so, commander.'

'You'll take it!' Kretschmer rasped. 'Otherwise we send someone else.'

Anders stared at the gun. It was an agonizing reminder of the time he had pointed the Luger at Weiner on *U700*'s bridge. Then he picked it up and said, 'I've got nothing to lose, have I? If I'm caught before I plant the bomb, the British will hang me. If I'm caught afterward, they'll hang me anyway. And if I manage to escape to Ireland after destroying the boat, the navy will hang me after the war.'

'Very likely,' Kretschmer observed.

Anders smiled thinly. 'Well at least I know where I stand.' He paused. 'When do I break out?'

'Is the harness finished?'

'Yes, commander.'

Kretschmer drummed his fingers. 'We already have some papers and clothing, but not a great deal of money. On the other hand, I see no point in delaying the mission. We go tomorrow night.'

58

In Lorient, Admiral Doenitz had just completed his inspection of the modified Ju52. He stood back from the aircraft and gazed at it, an expression of satisfaction on his sharp features. He pointed to the torpedo that was slung between the Junkers' undercarriage legs.

'Is it safe to leave the torpedo in position?'

'Perfectly, admiral,' Goder said. 'We won't fuel her until thirty minutes before take-off. That way we'll keep the strain on the undercarriage to a minimum.'

Doenitz returned to his Mercedes and sat silently for some moments. Kneller knew better than to disturb his thoughts.

'Has there been a change in the weather forecast, John?'

'None, admiral.'

'Very well. See that Gallagher receives his final instructions today.' Doenitz tapped his driver on the shoulder and turned to Kneller as the car moved off. 'Goder and Hartz will be taking off for Barrow tomorrow night.'

59

The following day, after the evening roll call, Anders entered the stable. The station wagon was there. The major worry had been that Lillian might decide to leave before her usual schedule.

A few minutes after Anders entered the stable, a small party of prisoners armed with buckets, chamois and hand mops, appeared at the upper windows that overlooked the stableyard and its approaches and set to work to make the windows shine. Another man was weeding the lawn in front of Lillian's sickbay. His job was to walk whistling through the stableyard after Lillian had closed her windows preparing to leave her office.

Faulk and Shulke sauntered into the stableyard deep in conversation. One of the window-cleaning lookouts cracked his chamois twice. The two men raced into the stable and pulled the door shut.

Anders was struggling into a crude, homemade webbing

harness similar in design to a parachute harness. 'The hooks are in place,' he said as Shulke helped him. 'I haven't had time to test them, but they ought to hold if she doesn't drive too fast.'

'She will,' Faulk said.

'Sssh!' Shulke put a warning finger to his lips.

There were footsteps outside. The door opened, and Kretschmer entered. 'All set?' he asked.

'Nearly,' Anders said. 'The bomb and greatcoat are in position.'

Kretschmer went down on one knee and looked under the station wagon. The shoebox bomb had been hidden in a stolen British kitbag and was hanging from a clip secured to the station wagon's chassis. A greatcoat, rolled into a tight pack, was also hanging from the chassis.

'Excellent,' Kretschmer said, straightening up. 'Maps and papers?'

'Sewn into the greatcoat's lining,' Anders said, pulling the curious harness tight around his body. 'Okay. I'm ready.'

Kretschmer held out ten pounds in banknotes and loose change. The coins had been individually wrapped to prevent them jingling. Anders thrust the offering into his pocket.

'Everyone contributed something,' Kretschmer said. 'Including Lieutenant Stein. And don't forget, Anders, if you can't get aboard the U-boat, place the bomb under the deck casing.'

Anders nodded. 'Commander,' he began hesitantly. 'I wondered if . . .'

'I can't make promises,' Kretschmer interrupted. Then his expression softened. 'But I'll give evidence for your defence.'

He held out his hand.

'Good luck, Anders. And write to us from Ireland.'

'I'd like you to have this,' Shulke said holding out a tiny, silver St Christopher medallion.

'Thank you, Conrad,' Anders said gratefully. 'You've been a good friend.' Then: 'Right. I'm ready.'

Five minutes later Anders lay suspended in the harness underneath the station wagon feeling like a trussed turkey. His cheek was pressed against the gasoline tank, one leg was hooked over the vehicle's propeller shaft, and the other was a few inches above the muffler. The lowest part of his body, his back, was less than nine inches from the ground. Already the harness straps were beginning to cut into his limbs and slow his circulation. He prayed that Lillian would not keep him waiting long.

'What are his chances?' Shulke asked as he, Faulk, and Kretschmer walked away from the stable.

'Of blowing up the U-boat?' Kretschmer said, drawing deeply on the last half-inch of his cheroot. 'About fifty-fifty.'

'Of reaching Ireland,' Shulke said.

'Zero,' Kretschmer said. He dropped the cigar butt and ground it into the cobbles with his heel.

Lillian closed the sickbay's sash window, pulled down the heavy blackout blind, and locked her door. She took off her uniform and looked sadly at her stockings. They would never do. Her last pair too. Slacks would solve the problem, but David detested them. The day was approaching when she would be forced to wear the army issue horrors – when she could get them. She sighed and rolled them off. On her desk was one of Oliver Lyttelton's 'make do and mend' pamphlets, issued by the Board of Trade, containing advice to young ladies dressing up for that 'important evening out'. Its tips on 'the amazing things that can be achieved with the circumspect application of an eyebrow pencil' were just short of hilarious. Giggling to herself, she positioned her mirror, and with infinite care, began drawing a stocking-seam black line up the back of her leg with an eyebrow pencil.

It was five minutes since Anders had heard the worm-cast remover strolling through the stableyard whistling the current hit tune *I Yi-Yi-Yi-Yi-I Like You Very Much*.

The strap was cutting cruelly into his legs, and his arms were numb. Of all the men throughout the country at that time who were waiting for women to get changed, his vigil was the most painful.

Lillian critically examined her false seams. Not bad. She pulled on the pair of hated panties that her mother had made for her from parachute silk. She always felt uncomfortable in them and the vivid display of blue sparks they produced when she took them off was unnerving.

Kretschmer looked at his watch in irritation. There was another hour of daylight left. The later the girl left, the better, but he was worrying about the effect the long wait would be having on Anders.

Sweat trickled into Anders' eyes, but there was nothing he could do about it. He tried to rub the side of his face against the petrol tank, but that only made matters worse. Perhaps she had decided not to go out after all – even if it was a fine evening. There was a faint sound. He stopped breathing and listened. It was the unmistakable clip-clop of high heels on cobblestones. They got louder and then stopped. There was the sound of a key being inserted in a lock. Anders' heart stood still. My God! The doors! They'd forgotten to lock them! There was a faint exclamation of surprise from Lillian when she discovered that turning the

196

key had locked the double doors. She unlocked them and pulled the doors open. Anders had a glimpse of her ankles as she walked down the side of the car and got in. Even with her slight weight, he was surprised at the amount the leaf springs settled.

The starter motor churned, then whined harshly as the engine fired once and kicked the Bendix pinion out of mesh. The engine started on the third attempt. There was a crunch from the gearbox. Anders had to move his right hand quickly to prevent his fingers from being caught in the handbreak linkage as it moved to release the rear brakeshoes. His body jerked suddenly as the car reversed out of the stable. A sharp pain in his calf reminded him to keep his leg off the propeller shaft's exposed universal joint. There were more crunching noises as Lillian tormented the gearbox into providing her with first gear. She revved up and released the clutch. The station wagon left rubber on the cobblestones as it shot out of the stableyard, narrowly missing a prisoner with slow reflexes.

The rapid acceleration threw a tremendous load on the shackles that supported Anders' weight. Horrified, he watched helplessly as the one that held the left side of his body slowly began to open. He desperately heaved his body to one side in an attempt to ease the burden on the shackle, but Lillian's hard cornering on the gravel drive leading to the main gate made the manoeuvre impossible. He was oblivious to the sharp stones that flew up from the tyres and peppered his face – all that concerned him was the terrifying thought that it was only a matter of seconds before the shackle gave way completely and dropped his tortured body onto the road.

Leymann and Shulke were pretending to be busy sweeping up leaves near the main gate when they heard the long-awaited sound of Lillian's station wagon. They continued working as the vehicle drew up in front of the steel gate. A soldier emerged from the guardhouse. Shulke bent down to gather up an armful of leaves and saw, to his horror, that one of the straps was trailing on the road behind the vehicle. And even worse – Anders had his hand on the ground and was struggling to push himself up.

'Evening, sweetheart,' said the soldier affably to Lillian, propping himself against the driver's door. Three times he'd asked Lillian out, and three times she had refused. But he wasn't one to give up that easily. 'He's done the brakes, then? All right now, are they?'

'Absolutely super,' said Lillian. 'Just a bit of a squeal from the back.'

The soldier looked concerned. 'Could be the shoes binding,' he said. 'Can make the drums overheat.' The soldier moved to the rear of the station wagon and started to kneel down by the rear wheel.

'I'm dreadfully late,' said Lillian impatiently.

'Won't take a minute.'

'Look, I haven't come a hundred yards. I'm terribly late, so if you don't mind opening the gate . . .'

The soldier decided he was wasting his time. After a cursory inspection of the car's interior, he signalled the corporal to open the gate.

Lillian stirred up some aggravation in the gearbox with the gear lever and hurtled through the gate, accelerating hard toward the 400-yard stretch of rough track that led to the main road. She loved fast driving – especially the weaving drive along the unmade road, swerving from side to side to avoid rocks and potholes without easing her foot off the throttle pedal. There was one particular jagged rock that jutted up at least nine inches. Since the expensive time when she had hit it, she had learned to position her hurtling car so that the rock passed between the offside wheels and the bulging centre of the rear axle.

60

The late afternoon sun sparkled on the Junkers' wings as the gang of mechanics wheeled it out of its hangar at Lorient. The aircraft was moved to a dispersal point where two gasoline tankers were waiting.

Goder and Hartz checked the flowmeters that measured the fuel as it was pumped into the Junkers; it was essential that they knew exactly how much gasoline they had aboard when the refuelling was complete.

With fuel gurgling into the aircraft's tanks, the two men completed their inspection of the cabin. The extra tanks that had been fixed to the floor looked satisfactory, and the stopcocks turned easily. There hadn't been time to install solenoid-operated fuel valves that could be controlled from the flight-deck; thus it would be necessary during the long flight to enter the cabin periodically to replenish the Junkers' ordinary tanks from the additional tanks by opening and closing valves manually.

Goder left the cabin and jumped down on to the concrete. The sun was still surprisingly warm as it had been all day. He walked into the shade of one of the gasoline tankers and looked up at a mechanic standing on a wing holding a gasoline hose steady.

Something was worrying Goder. There was a tiny but vital detail he was certain he had overlooked. It had been worrying him all afternoon, and he had been confident it would eventually come to him. But now, with less than two hours to take-off, he still could not think what it was.

61

Dusk was falling on the Cumberland fells by the time Gallagher was satisfied with the arrangement he had rigged so that he could transmit the homing signals to the Junkers without having to dismount from his motorcycle. He had lashed one of his fishing rods to a small haversack so that the rod with the antenna wire attached would be upright when he was wearing the haversack on his back. Such a short antenna would effectively reduce the range of the transmitter, but the Junkers ought to be in range from three hours before dawn when he was due to make his first homing transmission.

Homing, thought Gallagher wryly. That was a joke. Not only would his signals guide the Junkers to him, but also every bloody British soldier in north-west England. Holy Mother of God – riding around Barrow in the small hours of the morning! He wouldn't have to use his radio to arouse suspicions.

He checked the specific gravity of the motorcycle's battery with a hydrometer. He didn't want the battery to let him down at the last minute so that he would be forced to operate the transmitter with the motorcycle's engine running; he knew that he would need his ears more than any other sense in the back streets of Barrow.

He quickly packed his tent and cooking equipment and hid them in a foxhole. Tonight he would dine in Barrow and find himself a girl with a warm heart and a warm bed to rent.

62

Fleming recognized the station wagon that pulled out of the turning 200 yards ahead of his Bentley: it belonged to the crazy nurse who had tried to pass him when he and Brice had arrived in Cumberland.

Fleming's foot went to the floor. The Bentley's pistons increased their pounding and sent a great surge of power through the gearbox to the Brooklands thoroughbred's rear wheels.

Lillian heard the approaching howl of the Amherst Villiers supercharger and looked in her mirror. She smiled. It was the conceited naval commander. She accelerated and swung into the middle of the road. She wasn't going to let the arrogant oaf get past that easily.

63

It was dusk in Lorient when Kneller's phone rang.

Doenitz was standing some yards away looking out of a window, but he could plainly hear that the caller sounded extremely agitated.

'*What!*' Kneller said disbelievingly.

Kneller clapped his hand over the mouthpiece. 'It's Goder, admiral,' he said in a strained voice.

'Well?'

'He wants all the electric fans in the headquarters building to be put on a truck and sent to the airfield immediately.'

Doenitz lifted the electric fan off Kneller's filing cabinet and coiled the wire around the base. 'Tell him that he'll have every fan we can find in twenty minutes.'

Kneller swallowed. 'Shall I ask him why?'

'There'll be time for that later,' Doenitz said, moving quickly to the door. With that simple statement he demonstrated why he was an admiral and Kneller was not.

64

Lillian waved to Fleming as the Bentley swept past. Fleming gave her a languid salute, and Lillian watched the coupé receding along the coast road before she turned off the main road and drove up the deserted track that led to the secret spot on the cliffs.

She could see the roof of David's Austin 7 above the gorse bushes. He got out when he heard her car approaching.

65

At six o'clock, Doenitz's Mercedes arrived at the airfield and parked near the floodlit Junkers. Kneller gaped in astonishment at the aircraft, too stunned to move. Doenitz was already striding across the concrete, stepping over heavy electric cables that snaked toward the aircraft from a roaring generator truck parked nearby.

There were electric fans everywhere, trained on the

gasoline tankers standing by the Junkers. Some were positioned under the wings, blasting air upward at the wing fuel tanks, and several were actually on the wings training streams of cool air into open inspection panels.

'What the devil's going on?' Kneller muttered.

'I think I can guess, John.'

A mechanic passed the word to Goder that Doenitz had arrived. The pilot appeared in the Junkers' doorway. He jumped down and gave Doenitz an embarrassed salute. 'Thank you for sending the fans so quickly, admiral.'

Doenitz carefully moved around a dangerous looking tangle of electric wires and leaned into the aircraft's cabin. As he expected, there were more fans clustered around the fuel tanks. One mechanic was even placing wet towels on top of the tanks.

'Will someone tell me what is going on?' Kneller pleaded.

Goder was crestfallen. 'It was my fault. The gasoline tankers have been standing in the sun all day, and it's been exceptionally warm. The fuel warmed up in the tankers and expanded so that, although we'd filled Iron Annie's tanks to the brim, we couldn't pump the full weight aboard.'

Kneller immediately understood. Had the Junkers taken off loaded with warm fuel, it would have contracted rapidly as it cooled, depriving the aircraft of gasoline as effectively as if there had been a leak in every tank.

'How much longer will all this take?' Doenitz asked.

'We should be all right now,' Goder said. He signalled the generator truck to cut electric power.

A mechanic unscrewed one of the Junkers' gasoline filler caps and inserted a refuelling hose. Other mechanics did the same with the wing tanks. The gasoline tanker's pumps were switched on. Fuel could be plainly heard gushing into the Junkers' tanks.

'Ten minutes ago we filled the tanks up to the brim for the second time,' Goder said.

Five minutes passed before Goder announced that the Junkers had now received its full weight of gasoline. The portable floodlights and the electric fans were loaded on to a truck and driven away, followed by the gasoline tankers and the generator truck. The runway landing lights came on as Goder and Hartz shook hands with Doenitz.

A solitary fire engine drove across the airfield and waited expectantly halfway down the runway to one side. Doenitz and Kneller moved clear and watched Goder and Hartz walk around the big transport aircraft for a final visual inspection. Goder paid particular attention to the giant clamps that gripped the 21-inch torpedo between the undercarriage legs.

'We should have chalked a suitable message on the torpedo,' Goder commented as he followed Hartz aboard and closed the door.

The two men settled themselves in their seats. Goder checked that the three central throttle levers were back in the closed position so that the brakes were firmly on. He checked the magneto switches and turned the port engine over on the starter to prime the fuel injectors.

Goder smiled at Hartz as they went through the prestart procedure. 'Nervous?' Goder asked.

'Terrified,' the younger pilot admitted.

'You won't be now that you've got something to do.'

The port engine coughed, and within a few seconds all nine cylinders of the BMW engine were firing smoothly.

'Sweet as honey,' Goder said, repeating the procedure with the starboard and nose engines.

Once all three engines were checked and running correctly Goder, not wishing to waste fuel, immediately teased all three throttles forward to get the Junkers moving. The brakes came off but nothing happened. Only when all three counters were showing six thousand revolutions per minute did the grossly overloaded aircraft begin to roll.

There was an ominous creak from the undercarriage when the wheels passed over the first of the seams in the runway concrete.

'My God,' Hartz muttered to himself. He knew the feel of the Junkers well enough to be certain that it would never make it. Its normal take-off speed was around 55 knots. He and Goder had calculated that it would take at least 70 knots to generate enough lift to get the Junkers air-borne. Goder had placed a marker two-thirds of the way along the runway. If they weren't air-borne when they reached it, there was just enough runway left to shut down the engines and apply the brakes.

They passed the 400-metre marker with the air speed indicator showing a miserable 25 knots.

At 500 metres the Junkers was up to 35 knots.

There was another heart-stopping jolt as the Junkers hit an extra wide seam.

Forty knots. Just enough speed for Goder to bring the tail up to reduce drag. It also reduced lift by decreasing the wings' angle of attack, but speed was the all important factor.

Fifty knots. The fire engine was pacing the Junkers. The entire airframe shook as the wheels pounded over the seams.

Sixty knots. The throttles were wide open. All three engines were delivering their maximum 675 horsepower output. Goder's hand went to the trim wheel. He edged the flaps down and felt the familiar pressure in the seat of his pants that tells a pilot when his wings are developing lift.

Seventy knots. The seams were now punishing the aircraft with shuddering, sledgehammer blows at three-second intervals. More flap. Seventy knots. Tail too high. Bring it down a trifle. Eighty knots. That was the last marker that flashed by. Too late to stop now. Takeoff or bust. More flap . . .

The pounding stopped. The Junkers was air-borne. Goder held her level to build up more air speed and then gently pulled the big transport's nose up for a slow, fuel-conserving climb to eight thousand feet.

66

It was dark when Anders crawled slowly out from under Lillian's station wagon and sprawled exhausted on the grass. It had taken him fifteen minutes to disentangle his aching limbs from the harness – fifteen minutes of unremitting torture. As he lay on the grass, the events of the past hour were a confused whirl of images. There was the moment when he had just managed to drag the trailing strap out of sight before the soldier from the guardhouse saw it; the hideous charge along the unmade track where a boulder imbedded in the ground had missed him by centimetres; and lastly, the deadly chase along the road with his helpless body hanging precariously in the path of a thundering Bentley that was sitting on the station wagon's tail.

Anders listened carefully for some seconds. Lillian and David had disappeared over a small hillock.

He squeezed back under the station wagon, released the clips that secured the kitbag and the greatcoat, and dragged them behind him into the undergrowth.

He felt better after a short rest and was even able to obtain a bearing on the Pole star through a break in the clouds. He unrolled the greatcoat and pulled it on. It was of a similar colour and cut to the British navy's overcoat. It fitted reasonably well and at least it concealed his lacerated uniform.

He cleaned his face on handfuls of grass, swung the kitbag over his shoulder, and stumbled off in the dark toward the main road.

67

While Anders was trying to find his bearings on Cumberland Fells, Alan Brice was repositioning an inspection cover on the magnetic torpedo on *U700*'s bow torpedo room. Petty Officer Evans stepped through the watertight door holding a steaming mug.

'Coffee, Mr Brice.'

Brice gratefully accepted the drink, sipped cautiously and tried hard not to grimace.

'I made it just like you said, Mr Brice,' Evans said proudly. 'It *is* all right, isn't it?'

Brice put the mug down. 'Let's say that we've both made progress this week, Evans – me with my torpedo and you with your coffee.'

Evans grinned. 'Are you staying aboard for the test dive, Mr Brice?'

'I wouldn't miss it for the world.'

'Do you reckon she can go as deep as them gauges say?'

'No reason why not. It's an all-welded pressure hull so that there are no rivets to be forced in by water pressure – and it's made of the best Krupp steel.'

Evans looked doubtful. 'Ours creak and groan something horrible at two hundred and fifty feet.'

Brice smiled. 'So do ours. Don't worry, you'll be boasting about this to your grandchildren. What time do we leave?'

'Oh seven hundred,' Evans said.

68

Gallagher woke and was seized with panic. He groped in the darkness for his watch. A book fell off the bedside table, but the sleeping girl at his side didn't stir. Gallagher found the light switch. It was 2:30. He sank thankfully back onto the bed. He had never expected to fall asleep. He pushed back the covers and looked at the girl. He had found her in a pub near the docks. Her husband was in the army, she had said, and she didn't fancy the idea of joining the Land Army or working in a factory to find the money for the rent. Gallagher wondered how much rent she had to find each week for the dingy room with its worn linoleum floor covering and brown leaves wallpaper that had long gone out of fashion.

He rolled a five pound note into a cylinder and pulled back the covers. He gently teased the girl awake with the tip of the paper tube. She opened her eyes and tried to push Gallagher's hand away. He unrolled the banknote and held it up for her to see.

She groaned.

'Haven't you had enough for one night?' But she took the money. 'Shopkeepers can't stand fivers. Haven't you got anything smaller?'

Gallagher grinned and made a coarse reply. The girl sighed and braced herself.

69

Hartz walked his dividers across the chart and fixed the Junkers' position as 300 kilometres west of Ireland at fifty degrees twenty minutes north. He double-checked the position by means of the *Console* radio navigation beacon receiver that collected the signals through the direction-finding loop on the top of the Junkers' fuselage. He had a good fix. He wrote the position down, returned to his seat, and handed the slip of paper to Goder.

'Okay,' the senior pilot said. 'Time for a course alteration.'

Goder brought the Junkers' nose around until it was heading due north.

They were halfway to their destination.

70

The streets of the grey, granite town were deserted. Anders stepped into a shop doorway and looked carefully around before unfolding the map and striking a match. The road map was of no use in identifying the town. And yet it had to be Ulverston – there was no other town of a comparable size in the area. Anders hastily dropped the match when he heard a vehicle approaching. It was a baker's van with slitted black-out cowls over its headlights. The name on the side of the van had been painted over. It was the same with the shops. Place names and telephone numbers had been obliterated, and he hadn't seen one signpost that night. The British were very efficient.

He walked for another ten minutes, pausing now and then to search shop windows for clues. He saw a house with a plaque screwed to the wall near the front door. He crossed over, but the plaque, put up by a proud owner of the house, merely informed him that it was where Stan Laurel of the Laurel and Hardy partnership had been born.

He passed a telephone box. A hundred yards farther on he stopped, raced back to the box, and pulled the door open. He nearly dropped the matches in his excitement. The label in the centre of the dial had been removed and then unofficially restored by means of a strip of gummed paper. It proclaimed: ULVERSTON 234.

He was halfway to Barrow.

71

Gallagher sat on the edge of the bed smoking a cigarette. The girl had fallen asleep again clutching the five pound note. He looked at his watch – 3:30. Thirty minutes to his first scheduled transmission. He stood and pulled on his clothes, taking care not to wake the girl. He looked down at her and felt in his jacket pocket for his wallet. It contained one hundred pounds in assorted used notes. He hesitated. Why should he? What had the British ever done for him except kill his father? And yet the girl had done everything he had asked of her without complaint. He pulled the money out of the wallet and dropped it onto the pillow. She didn't stir when he drew the bedclothes over her shoulders and gently kissed her on the cheek.

He went quietly down the stairs and let himself out the backdoor. His motorcycle was leaning against the outside toilet. It took him ten minutes to connect the fishing rod and strap it to the haversack. He wheeled the machine down the passageway between the houses and pushed it a hundred yards along the street before swinging his leg over the saddle and kicking the starter.

Anders knew he was on the outskirts of Barrow because he had been able to identify a number of features from the map, and the advertisements in a newsagent's window had given mostly Barrow addresses. A truck was parked at the side of the road some twenty yards ahead. Anders thought it was deserted, but suddenly a door opened and the figure of a man was framed against the red glow of the softly illuminated interior. Anders was familiar with red lighting because it was used in U-boat control rooms at night to preserve the night vision of those going on lookout duty. The vehicle would be military. It was, in fact, an army wireless truck. Anders could see the direction-finding loop mounted on the roof, but it was too late to turn back. The soldier had sat down on the truck steps and was nursing a hot drink. He had seen Anders and was watching his approach with interest.

Hartz moved aft into the Junkers' cabin and opened the fuel cock on the main tank. The level in the sight glass sank as the fuel drained into the underfloor tanks. He yawned and rubbed his eyes. They had been flying for nine hours.

'Lucky swine,' muttered Corporal Anderson, eyeing Anders walking past the radio truck. 'Skulking back to his ship for breakfast. Navy types have all the luck.'

The captain slipped one of the headphones off his ear. 'Did you say something, corporal?'

'How much longer are we going to keep this up for, sir? Maybe he's gone home or changed his frequency?'

'Charlie One will hear him if he has, corporal,' was the captain's unsympathetic reply.

A motorcyclist rode by with a fishing rod and a haversack strapped to his back.

My God, thought the corporal. Bloody all-night anglers as well.

The corporal was now convinced that he was the only soldier in the north of England who wasn't getting time off.

Gallagher had spotted the direction-finding loop on the top of the truck. 'Holy Mother of God,' he muttered to himself. He prayed that the British weren't monitoring on the forty-eight metre band that night, but knowing his luck, they probably were. He held his watch in the meager beam of the hooded headlight: 3:45. Fifteen minutes to get to the docks and start work. He had plenty of time.

Hartz sat at the radio set, put the headphones on, and tuned the receiver to 48.1 metres. He wondered who the mysterious radio operator in Barrow was who would be guiding them toward their target.

The chart under his hand showed that the Junkers had flown virtually all the way around Ireland. In a few minutes Goder would make another eastward course correction. Hartz looked out of the window, but there was nothing to see but cloud. It had been like that all the way from France.

Gallagher coasted his machine to a standstill and listened. It was a typical dockland street with depressing rows of slate-roofed houses and warehouses that had been built nearly two centuries before during the Industrial Revolution. The entire area was the same – a maze of gloomy streets and grimy tenements with only gleaming brass door knockers and holystoned front steps to challenge the pervading air of squalor and deprivation.

Gallagher had spent two days getting to know the district – memorizing the names of every street and discovering where the back alleyways went to and which ones he could get the motorcycle through if he had to.

He looked at his watch. One minute to transmission. He sat upright on the saddle so that the antenna was perpendicular and reached for the horn button.

Hartz heard the soft bleeps in his headphones and quickly reached up to rotate the direction-finding loop. The operator transmitted five pulses at two second intervals. The broadcast lasted just long enough to get a bearing. He checked the angle of the loop and converted it to a true bearing. The Junkers was a mere two degrees off course.

'He's back!' yelled Corporal Anderson, almost knocking his headphones off as his arm shot up to crank the hand wheel that turned the direction-finding loop.

The captain grabbed the radio-telephone handset and spoke quickly to the other wireless truck.

'Bloody hell – he's stopped,' Anderson complained.

The captain looked surprised. 'So soon?'

'It wasn't a message, sir. Just blips, five of them. I got the last two at field strength eight from the docks area.'

'Field strength eight, corporal?'

Anderson grinned. 'That's right, sir. Sounds like we're right on top of the bastard.'

The captain stared at the corporal. 'Are you sure, corporal?'

'Positive, sir. I could even make out his morse key. Mushy make-and-break. Homemade or something.'

The captain tapped his teeth with a pencil. 'Charlie One didn't get his bearing,' he said thoughtfully. 'And if he didn't send a message, it's possible that he'll be talking again.' The captain reached for his radio-telephone. 'I think I'll notify General Bowen.'

Twelve minutes later two Bedford army trucks, each one carrying a small company of armed commandos, moved through the sleeping streets of Barrow.

Anders was hopelessly lost. Every street looked alike: endless rows of tenements, bow-fronted Victorian houses, and crumbling warehouses. He could hear heavy trucks moving in a nearby street and decided he had better hide until they had gone. The particular street he was in was about 300 metres long with a junction at each end. The road was curved so that by hiding in a doorway half way down the block, he would be able to keep both junctions under observation in case the trucks appeared.

He found an entrance to a narrow alleyway between two warehouses and crouched down, listening intently for the sound of the diesel engines. The trucks had either gone or stopped.

He was about to emerge from his hiding place when a motorcycle suddenly turned into the street. He pressed himself back into the alleyway as the machine roared past and stopped at the opposite end of the street.

Gallagher, unaware that he was being watched by an escaped German prisoner-of-war, cut his engine and listened. He felt a prickling sensation at the back of his neck as he watched the second hand of his watch – his finger poised on the horn button. He sensed that something was wrong and was tempted to abandon the next beacon or

214

move to another street. But it had to be this street because it was near the German U-boat and there was an alleyway that he could use as an escape route if both ends of the street were sealed off. Exactly fifteen minutes after his last transmission, Gallagher tapped out another five pulses.

He listened again. Silence. Then a starter motor churned a diesel engine into life. It was a long way off. There was no wind so it could be as much as a mile. It might be a coincidence that it had started so soon after he had finished transmitting, but it was the sort of coincidence that made Gallagher uneasy. He decided to make his next transmission from the opposite end of the street in case that wireless truck had obtained a good fix.

Corporal Anderson frowned at the map of Barrow. 'That's odd, sir. That last transmission came from a different area.'

'Sure you didn't make a mistake the first time, corporal?'

'Positive, sir.' The corporal stared at the map. 'Maybe he's mobile. That must be it! You ought to tell those commandos to be on the lookout for some kind of vehicle.'

By now Anders was convinced the motorcyclist was a policeman who was looking for him or knew that he was hiding in the alleyway and was playing a game with him. Anders got a grip on himself: the man was simply having trouble with his motorcycle. Or was he? Anders braced himself when the motorcyclist started his engine.

Gallagher swung his machine around and rode to the opposite end of the street. He stopped the engine and strained his ears into the night. Nothing. He checked his watch. A minute to the next beacon. Dawn in a couple of hours. A mist was rolling in from the sea. He blew on his hands. At least it didn't matter if they were cold because

215

he wasn't transmitting messages – just this accursed five pulse beacon every fifteen minutes.

He reached for the horn button. He got no further than transmitting two of the pulses because the diesel engines that burst into life sounded as though they were in the next street.

At first Hartz thought that the receiver had failed. He had picked up two of Gallagher's bleeps and no more. He rotated the loop antenna. Nothing. He tuned the receiver to Oslo, picked up a concert, and retuned back to the forty-eight metre band. There was nothing wrong with the radio receiver.

Gallagher kicked his machine into life and roared back to the opposite end of the street. He stopped, undecided what to do. He hadn't completed the transmission and was certain that the aircraft heading toward Barrow would continue to listen. By now the British were certain to know that he was mobile; so continuing to transmit from the same street might confuse them.

Anders heard a faint sound from the opposite end of the street to where the motorcyclist was waiting. He peered around the corner of the alleyway in time to see the darkened army truck coast to a standstill, its engine switched off. Soldiers armed with rifles jumped down from the vehicle's tailboard. They must have been wearing soft shoes, for their movements were soundless as they formed a line across the road.

Anders seized the kitbag and doubled back down the alleyway. He froze when he heard faint voices from the darkness at the far end of the passageway. They had the entire area sealed off. There was no chance of escape. He made his way back to the alleyway's entrance.

* * *

Gallagher started his machine and swung it in the direction of the waiting commandos. He didn't see the line of soldiers across the road until he was level with the entrance to the alleyway. Suddenly the street was filled with light from the truck's uncowled headlights.

'Halt!'

Gallagher slewed the machine around, kicked it into second gear, and roared back down the street in the opposite direction. A second army truck screeched across the road in front of him, its headlights adding their blazing beams to illuminate the trapped motorcyclist.

'Halt, or we fire!'

The alleyway was Gallagher's only hope of escape. He tore the blackout off his headlight and turned it full on. He spun the machine around in a skidding U-turn, dropped into first gear, and lay himself on the tank as he aimed for the entrance to the alleyway.

The sound of the motorcycle thundering toward Anders was deafening in the narrow passageway. Was the motorcyclist bent on killing him? He was too blinded by the headlight to climb the walls that lined each side of the alley. Suddenly there was the reverberating crash of sustained rifle fire. Bullets whined into the masonry above Anders' head. He dropped the kitbag and flattened himself against the wall just as the motorcyclist screamed and threw up his hands. His body seemed to be lifted from the saddle by the force of the bullets that ripped into him. His arms and legs flailed in the air. Then his body hit the ground, rolled over, and stopped within two yards of Anders. The riderless motorcycle produced a shower of sparks as its handlebars gouged along the brickwork, before falling on to its side, its back wheel spinning as the engine continued to race, and the headlight still burning.

Anders kept perfectly still, hardly daring to breathe.

The motorcyclist was motionless. But his eyes were open, and they were staring straight at Anders.

The motorcycle engine suddenly died, and a strange stillness descended. The cordite fumes from the soldiers' rifles mingled with the night mist that seemed to glow with ethereal light from the motorcycle's rear lamp.

Then there was a movement of khaki as four soldiers, led by a sergeant, moved quickly toward Gallagher's body. They were crouched low. Alert. Rifles at the ready. The sergeant dropped onto one knee by the still form, but there was no need for him to examine the body closely. He straightened up and saw Anders watching him with wide, frightened eyes. The sergeant stiffened, quickly brought his rifle up until it was pointing at Anders' chest, and jerked his head down the alleyway toward the trucks. Anders obediently moved off.

'Hey, you!'

Anders stopped and looked back. The sergeant was pointing at the kitbag that Anders had dropped.

Goder swore loudly when Hartz told him the signals from Barrow had ceased. Since picking up the first two beacons, they hadn't worried about maintaining a running fix on their position. Hartz returned aft and obtained a rough fix from three BBC stations. It couldn't be relied on because the BBC had erected small sub-transmitters near their main stations to prevent them from being used as navigation aids by the Luftwaffe.

Goder toyed with the idea of abandoning the mission and turning back. Without the homing signals they stood little chance of locating the U-boat. It was the thought of Doenitz's hard, grey eyes that made him decide to press on.

Anders stood by the truck while the commandos loaded the motorcyclist's body aboard. He was puzzled – the soldiers had caught him but weren't taking any notice of him. They seemed to be more interested in the dead man's motorcycle.

'You still here, mate?' It was the sergeant.

Anders blinked at him, not understanding.

'Submarines?' the sergeant asked.

Anders nodded.

The sergeant put a friendly arm around Anders' shoulder and steered him away from the truck. 'I expect you've seen worse. Best get back to your sub and forget it, eh?'

Stunned, Anders walked away from the scene. The sergeant watched the receding figure and shook his head sadly before turning back to his commandos and bellowing orders.

The two army trucks swept past Anders as he walked along the street. An arm waved from the leading vehicle. Anders kept walking blindly, wondering if they would suddenly return to arrest him. He had no idea where he was, but there was the unmistakable tang of salt water in the air. The trucks reached the end of the street and turned off. As they did so, their headlights swept across the large noticeboard outside a factory. To Anders, the three words on the noticeboard were the most important words in the world: VICKERS SUBMARINE WORKS.

Only the plant's main gate was guarded. Whistling a tune, Anders walked past the two dockyard policemen and reached the end of the road where a passageway led down the side of the plant. He climbed the chain link fence in the safety of the shadows and dropped behind a pile of marine gearbox castings. It was then that he heard the sound of lapping water. He dodged between piles of dockyard supplies and made his way toward the magic sound. He was crossing the railway track of a dockyard crane when a door opened nearby. He stepped back against a large crate. There were voices. Laughter. Footsteps on concrete. Anders carefully raised his head. The eastern sky was paling with the first tinge of dawn. Less than twenty yards away, the men were boarding a submarine. There was something hauntingly familiar about the dark outline of the conning tower.

And then Anders knew his search was over.

Moving silently, Anders found a flight of slippery steps cut into the quayside that led down to the water. He suppressed an involuntary shudder as the cold water rose around his body. The kitbag floated as it was supposed to do. He pushed it in front of him with his chin as he began the short swim toward *U700*.

Petty Officer Evans poked his cheerful face into the bow torpedo room where Brice was working.

'Morning, Mr Brice. Skeleton crew coming aboard. We're casting off in a couple of shakes.'

'How long before we reach the trials position?'

'Not for another four hours,' Evans said.

'In that case,' Brice said, hoisting himself on to a bunk, 'I think I'll get me a little sleep.'

Evans grinned. 'You do that, Mr Brice. We won't need to disturb you.'

Anders flattened himself against the conning tower under the overhanging wintergarten deck as two seamen untied the mooring ropes and cast off. They called to an unseen man on the bridge. The electric motors started, and the U-boat's stern began swinging away from the quay. Anders reached into the kitbag and groped beside the shoebox for the revolver. The two seamen were walking back along the deck casing to the bridge. Anders darted forward and crouched behind the main gun as they climbed on to the bridge. Had the officer on the bridge seen him, Anders was ready to hold him at gunpoint while winding the key that primed the bomb. But he wasn't seen. Thankfully Anders returned to the safety of the hiding place under the wintergarten deck to consider his course of action. The easiest way would be to prime the bomb and place it under the casing against the pressure hull. But if the British were taking the U-boat out to sea, it would be better to sink it in deep water where salvaging the boat would be difficult.

The early light revealed that *U700*'s course was westward – away from the dockyards, toward the open sea.

He decided to wait.

'So what do we do?' Hartz asked dejectedly.

'We'll have to carry on,' Goder replied. 'If we're on course, we'll be there in an hour. It's too late to think of turning back.'

Hartz looked down through his window at the mist rolling across the sea. The Junkers was flying east – toward the dawn.

'We won't find the U-boat in that fog,' Hartz said.

Goder smiled and gestured to the torpedo release lever between their seats. 'We're not going to waste that little beauty. We'll find a target.'

U700 was nearing the mouth of the estuary when Anders decided it was time to act.

The young officer hunched over the bridge coaming was about to give the order to switch the U-boat's electric motors over to the diesel engines, but his hand never reached the voicepipe cover. The cold muzzle of a revolver was suddenly thrust from behind into the side of his neck.

'Make no sound,' said a harsh, heavily accented voice. The officer looked down at the revolver and could see the gleaming noses of the bullets in their chambers. 'You understand?' The officer nodded.

221

Anders stepped back from the officer and kept the gun pointing at his chest. There was a fleeting recollection of the time he had pointed a gun at Weiner on this same bridge a lifetime ago. This time there would be no indecisiveness.

'You can swim?'

The officer hesitated then nodded. He climbed reluctantly down the ladder to the deck in response to Anders' gesture with the revolver.

'You give me cap and jacket.'

The officer removed his jacket and cap and dropped them at Anders' feet.

'Now swim.' Anders waved the revolver at the shore. 'Swim!' he repeated and pulled back the revolver's hammer.

The officer looked at the water creaming past the saddle tank and jumped.

Anders watched until the man had struck out for the shore before taking off his greatcoat and pulling on the officer's jacket and cap. He climbed down into the attack kiosk that was immediately above the control room and opened the locker that contained the Dräger submarine escape breathing sets. He lifted one up and looked at it critically. It consisted of an oxygen rebreathing bag that was connected by a short length of hose to a rubber mask that completely covered the wearer's face. The mask also distorted the wearer's voice.

Provided there were still smoke canisters in the deck ammunition lockers, Anders decided that it would suit his purpose admirably.

The two scientists and Petty Officer Evans spun around in astonishment as the young officer, wearing a breathing set, tumbled down into the control room.

'Fire! Quick!' Anders squawked. 'All on deck!'

'Where?' Evans demanded.

'On deck. Everyone! Quick! Quick!'

It sounded serious, and Evans wasted no time rounding the crew up and herding them to the ladder. 'There's just Mr Brice in the bow . . .' he began.

'On deck!' Anders interrupted, not understanding. Evans followed the crew up the ladder leaving Anders alone in the control room. Anders pulled off the breathing set and lowered the periscope so that it could be used in the control room instead of the attack kiosk. He grasped the handles and swung it around so that he could see the clouds of black smoke pouring out of the drainage holes from the canister. He had hidden the smoke canister under the extreme aft end of the tapered casing where the deck raked down to the foaming waterline. He smiled as he watched the men struggle to maintain a foothold on the narrow, slippery steel plate while they fought to connect an unwilling fire hose to a deck outlet.

The rest was easy. He stepped across the control room, spun the large helm wheel as quickly as he could, and grabbed a safety strap to keep his balance as the boat heeled violently. For the skeleton crew, there was nothing to grab but each other. When Anders returned to the periscope, the aft deck was deserted. Heads bobbed in the U-boat's wake. He hoped they could all swim.

He flipped the periscope to maximum magnification and studied the coastline. Five miles ahead, on the boat's starboard quarter, were heavily wooded slopes leading to low cliffs guarding a rocky headland. To the left of the headland was a small, sandy cove. Anders reasoned that if he exploded the bomb near the headland, not only would the proximity of the rocks make a salvage operation difficult, if not impossible, but he would stand a very good chance of swimming ashore at the cove.

He read off the course required to take the U-boat toward the headland and returned to the helm.

The captain of the coastguard station lowered his binoculars and stared out to sea. 'You'd better get on to Barrow,' he told his colleague. 'See if they've got a fast vessel with fire-fighting gear – their precious captured U-boat is on fire.'

There was slack water near the rocks. Anders went into the motor room and closed the sliding speed controls that shut down the electric motors. *U700* lost way and stopped.

The sudden silence in the U-boat woke Alan Brice. He sat up and yawned.

Anders went down on his knees in the control room and opened the hatch that gave access to the midships battery compartment. It was undoubtably the best place to position the bomb in order to blow the U-boat in two. He placed the revolver on the floor beside him and opened the shoebox. The six hand grenades were still neatly in place. He wound the alarm clock, which started ticking immediately, and set the mechanism to withdraw the pin from the priming grenade in two minutes. He was about to lower the bomb down the hatch when a shadow fell across him. He looked up.

'Now who in hell are you? Brice asked in surprise.

Anders went for the gun, but the American was too quick, kicking it out of reach. In desperation, Anders jumped to his feet and swung, but Brice ducked to avoid the blow and Anders' clenched fist collided with the hand-wheel. The sudden pain made him cry out. Before he could recover, Brice delivered a powerful blow that sank into Anders' stomach, and he collapsed to the floor, gasping for breath.

The alarm clock suddenly started buzzing. Puzzled, Brice picked up the shoebox. One glance as the turning alarm clock key pulled a pin out of a grenade was enough. He knew there were only seconds left. He raced up the ladder to the bridge and heaved the bomb overboard. The explosion from the priming grenade as the bomb hit the water threw Brice backward against the periscope standards. He struck his head on the torpedo aimer as he went down.

Hartz pointed excitedly at the distant plume of water that was rising into the air near the cliffs. Goder focussed his binoculars in time to see a second much larger explosion. The water settled enabling Goder to see that the explosions had taken place beside the stationary submarine that was close in to the cliffs. The submarine's profile was unmistakably that of a Type 7C U-boat.

With a whoop of triumph, Goder dropped the binoculars and put the Junkers into a dive. Hartz snatched up the binoculars. Not only did he pick out *U700*, but speeding toward it was a motor torpedo boat. It was some thirty kilometres from the U-boat but was moving fast enough to reach it in fifteen minutes.

'We've got it!' Goder yelled.

The three BMW engines screamed in protest as Goder hauled the Junkers out of the dive at 200 feet and slammed the throttles open to maintain the same air speed in level flight.

Anders ignored Brice groaning at his feet and stared at the nose-on profile of the airplane that was charging toward him at wave-top height. He was not going to let this Britisher stop him from destroying the U-boat. Not after he had got this far.

Anders pushed past Brice, jumped down to the wintergarten deck, and swung the multiple-barrelled gun down, centring the Junkers in the sights. He began to fire a continuous burst, shaking from the vibration of the yammering gun, half-blinded by the acrid fumes and deafened by the roaring of the murderously spewing barrels. Burning shell cases danced a staccato rattle on the deck plates and ricocheted off the safety rails. He could see the 20 millimetre tracer shells burning a path of light towards the Junkers. More elevation. Left. Too much. Right!

The Junkers was 300 yards from the U-boat when it flew into Anders' wall of flying lead and nickel. Bullets tore into the port wing's leading edge and chewed into the propeller blades, ripping the engine from the wing. The flight deck windows shattered and the instrument panel dissolved into shards of metal and flying splinters of glass.

Hartz was killed instantly by a tracer that lanced through his chest like a comet. Goder outlived his copilot by only seconds – but it was long enough to operate the torpedo release control before his body slumped forward.

Brice climbed to his feet, suddenly riveted by the spectacle of the Junkers cartwheeling into the sea, throwing up huge clouds of spray. The starboard wing climbed lazily into the sky, twisting and pirouetting like a sycamore seed, its black crosses flashing mockingly at Anders.

'No!' Anders said in German, his face white with shock. *'It's not possible!'*

Brice pointed at the water. 'Torpedo!' A corner of his mind noted that it was an old-fashioned 'heater' torpedo that left a track of compressed air bubbles, and the track was speeding straight for *U700*.

Brice braced himself for the explosion, but it never came. He swung around and saw that the torpedo had passed underneath the U-boat and was now streaking toward the cove 200 yards away. As he watched the wake of bubbles, the torpedo suddenly porpoised to the surface. Brice guessed that its momentum, when it hit the water, had carried it too deep and that it had only now picked up its correct running depth. The torpedo reached the shore, plowing through the surf, and several yards up the steep beach, its contra-rotating propellers whirring impotently.

A dud, Brice reasoned. Had the torpedo been equipped with a magnetic warhead, it would have exploded as it passed beneath the U-boat.

In the silence that followed, Brice heard the muted roar of the approaching MTB and suddenly remembered the other man on deck. He spun around, but it was too late. He felt himself falling back to the deck as Anders pushed by and scrambled down the hatch, pulling it shut behind him.

After a minute's destruction with a heavy wrench in the control room, Anders realized the futility of what he was doing. He sank to his knees in despair amid the wreckage of smashed gauges and valves. A small engraved identification plate caught his eye: TORPEDO DIREKTOR.

Anders stared at it for some moments. 'The spare warhead,' he whispered to himself.

Brice gave up trying to open the hatch and turned his attention to the MTB. The high-speed vessel marked by two clouds of spray on either side of its flared bows was now about four miles from *U700*.

Anders stopped hauling the hoist in the bow torpedo room when the nose of the warhead hanging from the rope was high enough above the floor to be certain of detonating when it fell. Next he piled virtually every flammable item he could find beneath the swaying warhead; curtains, mattresses, blankets, papers – anything that would burn was added to the mounting pyramid. He worked at feverish speed, aware that the MTB would be closing fast. The cheroot given to him by Kretschmer at *U700*'s commissioning party fell off his bunk as he dragged the mattress away. He spared it a cursory glance before thrusting it into a pocket. He found a large can of cleaning fluid and sprinkled the contents over the pyre and the interior of the torpedo room. He checked to make sure he had a box of matches and reached up to release the clips that secured the torpedo loading hatch.

When Brice saw Anders emerge through the hatch near the bow and fumble with a box of matches, he vaulted over the wintergarten rail and raced along the deck casing. Anders was about to strike the match when Brice was upon him, scattering the matches on the spray-drenched deck. Exploding with fury and frustration, Anders yanked the Webley out of his belt and squeezed off a shot. Brice dived sideways but the bullet hit his arm below the elbow. He gave a cry of pain and just managed to keep himself from tumbling into the water by grabbing the jumping wire with his free hand.

The MTB was less than quarter of a mile away, with a boarding party mustered on deck, together with the crew of the U-boat that the MTB had stopped to pick up.

Half crying, half cursing, Anders found the box of matches. There was one match left. Please be dry, he prayed. Please God make it dry and stop my stupid fingers from shaking!

He struck the match, dropped it down the hatch, and threw himself clear of the opening in time to avoid the huge tongue of flame that blasted into the air. It would be a matter of minutes before the fire burned through the rope causing the warhead to fall.

Brice stared at the blazing hatch, unable to credit his senses. The pain in his arm and the blood soaking into his shirtsleeve were forgotten. 'My notes!' he cried. He started forward as if by some miracle he hoped to extinguish the inferno.

Anders grabbed him by the shoulders and pointed to the cove. 'Ashore!'

Brice shook his head as if he didn't understand. Anders pushed the revolver more firmly into his waistband, hooked his arm around the American's waist, and jumped, dragging Brice into the water with him. The two men came spluttering to the surface.

'My arm,' Brice choked, fighting for air. 'I can't swim!'

Anders grasped Brice by the shirt collar and struck out for the cove.

The MTB cautiously approached the blazing U-boat. A firefighting party broke out a hose and directed the water jet at the flames leaping from the U-boat's forward hatch.

Another fire hose was brought into use, and together they succeeded in turning the flames to smoke and then to hissing steam. The MTB moved alongside the U-boat but was taking no chances – the hoses continued to blast water through the open hatch.

Anders stopped swimming and discovered he could stand. He helped Brice to his feet, and they staggered through the surf, finally collapsing on to the beach. Brice clutched at his arm in an attempt to stanch the flow of blood, and Anders saw the stain spreading into the sand. 'I'm sorry,' he said. He stood up and dejectedly watched the U-boat. There was only a wisp of smoke coming from the hatch. A seaman from the MTB scrambled down on to the U-boat's deck and approached the open hatch.

Brice called to Anders and pointed to the top of the low cliff above the cove. The two army trucks that Anders had encountered that morning in Barrow had emerged from the trees. Armed soldiers led by the sergeant were jumping down on to the grass. Anders was certain they would kill him just as they had killed the motorcyclist. Forgetting Brice, he raced to the foot of the cliff and started to climb the debris of stones and boulders that an old rock fall had piled against the bottom end of the cliff. 'Stop!' a voice yelled from above, but Anders kept climbing toward an overhang. A bullet chipped splinters from a nearby boulder, and Anders dived behind an outcrop, pulling out the revolver. He had five shots with which to give a good account of himself. He saw a flash of khaki near the top of the cliff and fired at it. Two more shots ricocheted off the boulder he was crouching behind. He didn't hear the sergeant drop down on to a nearby rock.

'Drop it, sonny!'

Anders swung the revolver around to the voice. The sergeant fired. The bullet slammed through Anders' stomach and sprayed the rocks behind him with bone and tissue.

The seaman dropped down into *U700*'s bow torpedo room and stared numbly at the blackened warhead hanging nose down from the charred remains of a rope. One by one the few remaining strands of rope were parting under their half ton load. The seaman senselessly threw his arms around the torpedo warhead and held it in a futile bear hug. But the torpedo fell.

Anders lived just long enough to see the explosion that blew the bows off the U-boat and tossed the MTB on to its beams ends as if it had been a toy. *U700* lifted its propellers high into the air. The conning tower disappeared as the boat rolled on to its sides. Then there was nothing but a swirl of sluggish bubbles erupting in the middle of the spreading oil slick that marked the spot where *U700* had submerged for the last time.

72

The soldiers were dismantling the cliff rescue winch when Lillian and Major Veitch arrived. The sergeant escorted them to the back of the truck and pulled back the blanket covering a stretcher.

Lillian nodded, her face pale. 'Yes,' she said quietly. 'That's him.'

'He had a gun,' the sergeant said. 'I didn't have no choice. It was him or me.'

'I understand,' Veitch said.

The sergeant held out a manilla envelope. 'Things we found on him. Personal things. There was a map, but that's got to be sent to GHQ.'

Lillian took the envelope. 'I'll see that they're sent to his people.'

73

Major James Veitch hated having to lie. He looked fixedly down at his blotter so that he wouldn't have to meet the expressionless eyes that were staring at him.

'He was found hiding in a shepherd's hut,' Veitch said

awkwardly, 'not three miles from the camp, by two Home Guard . . .'

'*Armed* Home Guard?' Kretschmer queried.

'Yes. But he broke away from them. They called out several times for him to stop, but he took no notice. One of them fired with the intention of wounding him but the shot went high.' Veitch paused. 'He died before the doctor arrived on the scene. The funeral is to be held in Hawkshead village. I'm prepared to grant parole to those officers who wish to attend on condition that they agree to wear British navy greatcoats over their uniforms to avoid annoying the villagers.'

'Thank you, major,' Kretschmer said tonelessly.

'Nurse Baxter will let you have his things to send to his family,' Veitch said and then paused. 'I don't expect you to tell me how he escaped, so I won't insult you by asking.'

The two men stood and exchanged salutes. Kretschmer was about to open the door to leave when Veitch spoke.

'Commander . . .'

Kretschmer turned.

'It was a courageous attempt,' Veitch said. 'He was a brave officer.'

Lillian sat down in her sickbay and tipped Anders' few possessions onto her desk. There was a silver St Christopher medal and a wallet containing limp, seawater-stained photographs of his parents. The remains of an unsmoked cheroot puzzled her, for she had never seen Anders smoke. She looked up and saw the lean figure of Kretschmer walking across the lawn toward the hall. She guessed that he was coming to collect Anders' things and quickly swept them into her drawer rather than let the German officer see that she had been looking at Anders' photographs.

She heard his footsteps outside in the corridor and

braced herself. She was frightened of the U-boat commander, and she suspected that Kretschmer was aware of her fear.

There was a tap on her door. It opened.

'I've come for Lieutenant Anders' belongings,' Kretschmer said.

Without looking up, Lillian said, 'I'll have them sent to your office, commander.'

Lillian took a deep breath as Kretschmer was about to close the door. 'I'm terribly sorry about what happened to Bernard – I mean – Lieutenant Anders,' she stammered. She looked up and met the unblinking eyes. Her courage ebbed away. To cover her embarrassment she blurted out what was on her mind: 'I suppose as you're a sailor – a fighting man – one more death doesn't . . . doesn't . . .' She groped for the right word, but Kretschmer interrupted her.

'One more death is always one more too many. Whether it's a man, or woman, or children – or a nurse in a lifeboat.'

Lillian looked up sharply into the piercing eyes, searching for a clue to the thoughts that lay behind them.

'You mean you've known all along?'

Kretschmer nodded slowly. 'She was your sister?'

'Yes,' Lillian said. 'How did you know?'

'There's a likeness. Also we picked up a list that gave the names of the passengers aboard the *Walvis Bay*. There was an army nurse. Elaine Baxter.'

'She died of exposure,' Lillian said dully.

'I'm sorry,' Kretschmer said.

'And you've known all along,' Lillian repeated disbelievingly.

'Her face was among the living,' Kretschmer said. 'They're the ones I always try to remember.' He paused.

'You must excuse me – I have to see about the details for the funeral.'

Lillian listened to his footsteps receding down the corridor. She opened the drawer and stared down at the small, sad collection of Anders' possessions. For five minutes she was undecided. She picked up the cheroot and studied it before finally making up her mind. There was an envelope and notepad in her drawer. She wrote 'Lieutenant-Commander Otto Kretschmer' on the envelope and placed the notepad in front of her.

It took her ten minutes to write a full account of what she knew about the destruction of *U700*.

74

Stein's face went white. He rose to his feet and stared contemptuously at Kretschmer, Leymann, Faulk and Shulke.

'Sit down, Stein,' Kretschmer said quietly.

Stein pushed his chair under the table. 'You ask me to be a pallbearer for a coward. The answer is no.'

'I said, sit down.' Kretschmer's voice was very quiet and very dangerous.

'Let the British carry his coffin. He's done more for them than he has for Germany.'

'We all share the responsibility for his death, Stein.'

'Not me,' Stein said. 'He lived like a coward and he died like one – running away. Don't go blaming me for his death, commander.'

'I don't want the British guessing the reason for Anders' escape,' Kretschmer said. 'Which they might do unless we show respect for a brother officer.'

Stein sneered. 'Suspect what? Anders buried that bomb as soon as he was out of the camp. He was a coward, and I don't go to the funerals of cowards.'

Kretschmer stood and faced Stein. 'If you don't do exactly as I say, Stein, I shall have no hesitation in notifying Major Veitch that your political views are such that you would be happier at one of the camps run by the Poles.'

'What political views?' Stein asked politely.

'The ones I saw you sharing with some of your SS friends at *U700*'s commissioning party.'

Stein stared at Kretschmer with sudden understanding. 'I was to have joined your boat . . .'

'That's right,' Kretschmer agreed. 'Except that I asked the admiral to find someone else. I didn't want you then. Just as I don't want you in this camp now unless you obey my orders without question.'

75

As Anders' coffin was lowered into the open grave, Major Veitch glanced around the churchyard and signalled to the bandmaster who was stationed with his musicians some thirty yards from the graveside. Two pipers detached themselves from the bank and took up positions beside the grave. The band started playing a piece of music that it was hard to imagine would ever be played in an English country churchyard during those dark days of October 1941 when Britain stood alone.

It was the German national anthem.

Major Veitch stepped forward and carefully lifted the White Ensign from the coffin. Underneath lay the German navy's battle ensign. Kretschmer was deeply moved by the simple gesture. He stood by the grave, bareheaded, holding his cap. Like his fellow officers gathered in the churchyard, he was disturbed and puzzled as to why the British had gone to such pains to provide Anders with full military honours.

The canon intoned a simple prayer and threw a handful of earth onto the coffin.

Kretschmer picked up a spade and helped shovel the earth into the grave. Then there was another surprise as six commandos led by a sergeant formed two lines near the graveside. They presented arms in response to the sergeant's orders and fired a three volley salute into the air over the grave.

Kretschmer turned to Major Veitch. He had difficulty in speaking. 'On behalf of all the officers at Grizedale Hall, major, I would like to thank you for all you have done for Lieutenant Anders.' He put his cap on and saluted.

The funeral was over.

A grey Bentley coupé pulled up outside the churchyard. Commander Ian Fleming got out and opened the passenger door for Alan Brice. The American scientist's right arm was in a sling. Fleming removed a large wreath from the car's trunk and gave it to Brice. The two men stood near the lych-gate and waited for the funeral party to leave the churchyard.

Kretschmer was the last man to climb aboard the army truck. The guard slammed the tailboard and latched it. Lillian crossed the road to the vehicle as the driver started the engine.

She was holding a manilla envelope, which she held up to the German officer.

'They're Bernard's things, commander. They were found on him.'

The truck started to move off. 'Thank you, nurse,' Kretschmer said politely. He was puzzled by her concerned expression.

Lillian kept pace with the truck. Her face was worried and drawn. 'I should have given them to you earlier, commander,' she said anxiously. 'Please don't tell anyone that I left it so late.'

'Of course not,' said Kretschmer, not looking at the envelope.

Lillian had to break into a trot as the truck gathered speed. 'You won't tell anyone,' she begged. *'Please, commander.* I could get into serious trouble.'

Lillian stopped running and watched the receding vehicle. Kretschmer gazed back at her with a bewildered expression on his normally impassive face.

Brice carefully laid his wreath on the grave beside the posy of flowers that Lillian had placed there moments before. He stepped back and saluted with his left hand while Fleming looked on.

The two men didn't speak until they were back in the car.

'The U-boat's lying in shallow water,' Fleming said. 'They'll have a good look at her today. It's possible that she'll be raised. Nothing left of the torpedo though. Or your notes.'

'I can remember the important details,' Brice said.

The army truck ground slowly up the steep fell that overlooked the village and its tiny graveyard.

Kretschmer opened the envelope and looked inside. He took out the remains of the cheroot and recognized it as one of his. He shook the contents of the envelope onto his lap – some photographs, ruined by seawater as the cheroot was, a wallet, and a letter. It was addressed to him in a woman's handwriting.

He opened the envelope and unfolded the single sheet of notepaper. The letter was unsigned. Leymann, sitting opposite Kretschmer, noticed that the colour was draining from Kretschmer's face. Kretschmer looked up from the letter and stared at the dwindling graveyard. For a moment it seemed to Leymann that Kretschmer was unable to speak. Then: 'Stop the truck!'

The driver braked. Ignoring the guards, Kretschmer jumped down to the road and stared down at the distant graveyard. He could see the splash of colour of a wreath. Slowly, he brought his right hand up to his forehead.

The chill October wind sweeping across the desolate fells caught at his greatcoat. Kretschmer stood motionless for a long moment. For the first time in his life, he wished he were a weaker man so that he might weep.

Postscript

On June 8, 1962, Lieutenant Bernard Anders' body was removed from the churchyard at Hawkshead in the presence of his family and re-interred in the German War Cemetery at Cannock Chase in England.

Ian Fleming died two years later; he was James Bond's only flesh and blood victim.

Otto Kretschmer married after the war and retired from the West German navy in 1957, having reached the rank of rear admiral.

Karl Doenitz succeeded Hitler to become head of state for twenty days before the final collapse of the Third Reich. He and his cherished U-boat arm were cleared of accusations of war crimes, but he was tried at Nuremburg for training men for war in peacetime and, perhaps unjustly, found guilty. He served a ten-year sentence at Spandau.

Alan Brice is retired and lives with his wife on Long Island. His three grandsons think that he's the best baseball pitcher in the world, although his performance does suffer on those days when his right arm troubles him.

A Selected List of Fiction Available from Mandarin Books

While every effort is made to keep prices low, it is sometimes necessary to increase prices at short notice. Mandarin Paperbacks reserves the right to show new retail prices on covers which may differ from those previously advertised in the text or elsewhere.

The prices shown below were correct at the time of going to press.

☐	7493 0003 5	**Mirage**	James Follett	£3.99
☐	7493 0005 1	**China Saga**	C. Y. Lee	£3.50
☐	7493 0009 4	**Larksghyll**	Constance Heaven	£2.99
☐	7493 0012 4	**The Falcon of Siam**	Axel Aylwyn	£3.99
☐	7493 0018 3	**Daughter of the Swan**	Joan Juliet Buck	£3.50
☐	7493 0020 5	**Pratt of the Argus**	David Nobbs	£3.50
☐	7493 0025 6	**Here Today**	Zoë Fairbairns	£3.50

TV and Film Titles

☐	7493 0002 7	**The Bill III**	John Burke	£2.99
☐	7493 0055 8	**Neighbours I**	Marshall/Kolle	£2.99
☐	423 02020 X	**Bellman and True**	Desmond Lowden	£2.50
☐	416 13972 8	**Why the Whales Came**	Michael Morpurgo	£2.50
☐	7493 0017 5	**Adventures of Baron Munchausen**	McKeown/Gilliam	£2.99

All these books are available at your bookshop or newsagent, or can be ordered direct from the publisher. Just tick the titles you want and fill in the form below.

Mandarin Paperbacks, Cash Sales Department, PO Box 11, Falmouth, Cornwall TR10 9EN.

Please send cheque or postal order, no currency, for purchase price quoted and allow the following for postage and packing:

UK	55p for the first book, 22p for the second book and 14p for each additional book ordered to a maximum charge of £1.75.
BFPO and Eire	55p for the first book, 22p for the second book and 14p for each of the next seven books, thereafter 8p per book.
Overseas Customers	£1.00 for the first book plus 25p per copy for each additional book.

NAME (Block Letters) ....

ADDRESS ....

....